BAYLYN, BEWITCHED

by

Christine Cacciatore
and
Jennifer Starkman

Book One of the Whitfield Witch Series

This book is licensed for your personal enjoyment only. This book may not be resold or given away to other people. If you're reading this book and did not purchase it, or it was not purchased for your use only, then please purchase your own copy. Thank you for respecting the hard work of these authors.

Copyright 2013 by Christine Cacciatore and Jennifer Starkman

Book cover designed by Tugboat Design

This is for my family of cheerleaders, who never once doubted my dream. I love you.

JS

To my three kids, for having faith in me. And for Joe, who told me I could do it until I finally believed him. I love you guys.

CC

To our Mom with love
CC & JS

Chapter 1

"She wants *what?*" Baylyn gawked at her co-worker. The small town library was half hour from closing when their biweekly order came in via email from a certain patron; namely, The Missus Dolores Billings.

"You heard me." Cat muffled her snicker behind her list of books. "She wants the last five issues of Popular Mechanic, a book called *Friend or Foe: What's Growing in YOUR Garden*, and also, you'll love this, all three books from the newest erotica series."

"All three?" Baylyn rolled her eyes. "Every time I think her requests can't get any weirder, she proves me wrong."

Tapping expertly on her computer keyboard, she furrowed her brow as she recited, "Hmm, the new series is all checked out. She's going to have to go on the waiting list. The others – I can do three issues of Popular Mechanic and that plant book? This might be the first and last time it's ever been checked out. She's in luck on that one."

She cast a grin towards Cat. "What could she possibly want with these?" Her requests made the oddest combinations.

Every other week was definitely a trip to Weird Land when the reclusive homebound old woman put several books on request. At first they thought it was a prank because of how varied the requests were, but they both learned to look forward with morbid curiosity to what was going on the hold list this time.

Tucking a long dark curl behind her ear, Baylyn's blue eyes widened as she exclaimed to Cat, "Holy cow, the wait on erotica set of books is over 60 days? They're probably doing a brisk business on neckties at the mall these days; what do you want to bet?" They both giggled.

Cat went back to shelving books and left Baylyn, Senior Librarian, up front. Baylyn, 29, average height, softly built without being plump, had long, dark hair with a wave in it that most girls would envy. Nine times out of ten, she had cat's eye glasses on for reading and people would almost catch their breath when she made eye contact with her baby blues.

She favored long, men's style shirts that she could belt over tweed skirts and tights; as for the traditional witch's garb of long black dresses, black nylons, those ridiculous high pointy witch hats and their equally ridiculous pointy uncomfortable heels? Perhaps on Halloween.

Baylyn was a witch, indeed, but flats and cute little cardigans were fine with her, thank you very much.

A familiar patron made his way up to the front to check out. Ben Davis was a middle aged man, with messy professor type hair and oversized, outdated glasses. He also had a massive crush on Baylyn...

...Who did not return the affection. However, she was always pleasant without being encouraging. She greeted him warmly. "Hi, Ben. Find everything you need?"

His cheeks pinked as he nodded, all the while trying not to stare at Baylyn and failing miserably.

His library card was on his key ring, and his hands shook as he handed it to her, dropping the keys on the desk.

"Sorry." He gave a nervous sigh. His discomfort was palpable.

"Don't worry about it." She gave him a gentle smile and finished checking out his books.

"Well, there you go." Long pause. She patted his stack of books and pushed them a bit toward Ben. She looked over his shoulder at Cat, standing at the door to leave and covering her mouth with her hand to stifle her laughter.

He pushed his glasses up his nose a bit and stared at her, smiling shyly.

"Ok, here you go; you're all set." Uncomfortable silence settled in at the circulation desk. She pushed the books towards him a bit more.

They were dangerously close to falling off the desk edge. He didn't seem to take the hint, the poor man. This had happened before.

She cleared her throat. "Was there something else I could help you with?"

Ben finally had the presence of mind to grab his books and, backing up slowly, he worked up the courage to wave at her weakly as he left.

Baylyn looked over to Cat, who was trying hard not to laugh at their lovelorn patron. "Poor guy. I'm surprised he got the keys to you this time." Baylyn smiled as she began straightening the desk.

"Isn't it about time for you to clock out for the night, smarty?"

"Okay, okay. Don't get your panties in a bunch. Just teasing you a bit. You want me to lock up the front?"

Laughing at her friend's expression, Baylyn spun around in her chair to look at the huge clock that hung from the entrance hall of the library. "No, there's still about six minutes left. Wouldn't want any nasty 'the library was closed' phone calls tomorrow. I'll do it in a few minutes. I'll see you tomorrow, though."

She began closing down the computers and decided she could use the last few minutes to shelve books. Ben had been the last patron of the very quiet night, and it would be nice to start the day with a clean cart. She wheeled the cart of books to the stacks and began examining the spines to put the books away.

Lost in thought, she belatedly registered the tone signaling a patron had entered the library.

"Oh, I'll be right there. Welcome to the library. We'll be closing in just a few minutes." She briskly found the correct spots for a couple of books she was holding.

In the distance she heard, "All right, then."

At the sound of his voice, all air stilled and suddenly she felt very odd. In the air she could feel a static charge and became aware of a very low level hum, almost below what she could register with her ears. Almost.

What was that? She looked at the spine of the next book, slowly, barely seeing it, when out of the corner of her eye she caught a dark, feathery shadow.

She gasped and her heart sped up as she snapped her head around to see what it was, only to realize it was her *hair*. She hadn't been just sensing a static charge—her long hair was rising up off her back and shoulders to stick out horizontally, obeying the presence of the static in the air.

All at once, she felt different. More *aware*. Her breath started to come a little faster as she attempted to smooth her hair down. She peeped around the shelf, trying to get a glimpse of the mysterious man moving around her library. The static, the vibrating hum—that had only started after he came in!

Try as she might, she could only catch glimpses of him, a tantalizing view of the dark curls on the back of his neck here, a delayed whiff of his cologne there, a strong hand gripping the bookshelf as he rounded the corner.

Baylyn moved this way and that trying to get a better look at him.

Suddenly, tik! tik! tik! She heard a rhythmic popping noise coming from the area around her desk. It took a second to register but she realized that it was the electric stapler on her desk misfiring over and over, all by itself. *What was going on in here?*

Still very aware of the low vibration running through the library, she fought again to smooth down the defiant black locks that insisted on residing horizontally on her head rather than vertically as she hurried her way through the library to her desk. She didn't want that stapler misfiring into her last library patron of the night.

The moment she reached the desk, the stapler stopped. Her hair floated softly back down to lay obediently on her back and shoulders once again.

She looked around, puzzled. What had that been all about? She shook her head as she collected the stray staples she found on the desk and threw them away, then patted down her hair again for good measure.

"We're closing in two minutes." she called out, looking around to see if anyone else had witnessed the odd goings on at the circulation desk.

"Right. I'll be there in a jiffy." His voice was deep and not one she recognized. In such a small town, working in a small library, there wasn't much of a chance to meet anyone new; the same people used the library all the time. But this! The dark hair, strong hands, cologne that was making her knees weak.

Someone new. A *male* someone new.

Almost as if on cue, the weird thrum started up again. She looked around, puzzled. Baylyn gave a little scream when the apparently possessed stapler began firing again. Ping! Ping! Ping! The chattering teeth Cat had confiscated from an unruly youngster earlier began to clack together loudly.

Now how is that possible? They weren't even wound up! She tossed down the stapler and grabbed for the teeth and as she did, she could feel her hair lifting up off her neck again, to stand out belligerently a la Pippi Longstocking.

A deep male voice came from behind her.

"Excuse me, Miss. I need to make some copies but it looks like your copier is on the fritz."

Startled, and rattled by all the apparent poltergeist activity occurring all around her, Baylyn whirled around to match a face to the deep, pleasing voice.

In doing so, she got her first full look at Declan Hughes. He was tall and muscular without shouting "gym rat". His piercing blue eyes were ice blue. It was almost difficult to look into them.

His scent. He smelled like nothing she had ever breathed in. He smelled of sunshine and pine, all topped off by an irresistible, unique, *man* smell.

Baylyn simply stared at him with her mouth slightly open, hair standing straight out on either side of her head. The electric stapler ran out of ammunition to spit and flipped on its side, seizing weakly. The chattering teeth managed to get in a few more clacks before she used both hands to hold the jaws together. She vaguely recognized that she must look like a fool. Had she the composure, she would have used her hand to push up her *own* jaw.

She drank in the sight of him, her soft blue eyes meeting his direct gaze, then dropping to his strong mouth that was currently curved into a smile.

The silence stretched out yet she felt powerless to move or even speak.

Say something, she begged herself. *Anything. SPEAK!!*

She swallowed convulsively. "I can do you."

No. No, no. She could feel her face reddening profusely. *Please tell me I didn't say that out loud.*

She closed her eyes in embarrassment and tried again. "I can do that for you."

Behind her, the stapler toppled right off the desk.

Chapter 2

Well, well, well. Things in Whitfield just got a little bit more interesting, thought Declan as he stroked his chin thoughtfully, and sat in his brother Devin's luxurious office the next morning inside the Hughes and Sons building.

Scratch that...a *lot* more interesting. Who would have thought that in a library, a dry, dusty library for goodness sake, he would find such an interesting and beautiful creature?

Bay Travers. The long, dark curly hair and eyes that had looked right into his soul. Looked right in and captured it.

Careful, he warned himself. *Pretty is as pretty does.* He had learned that lesson well, not that long ago.

He heard female voices outside his office. "Are you kidding me? Well, I heard..."

"Oh, I would totally show him around town..."

Declan shook his head and rolled his eyes. He wanted only one person to show him around town. Not that he needed the help, having grown up two towns over, but her delightful company—now that would be something.

He stirred another creamer into the bitter cup of coffee he ended up with when he tried to make a pot. He listened to the bits and pieces of gossip outside his closed-but-not-shut office door.

Unbeknownst to them, however, the object of their gossip was sitting not ten feet from where they were whispering. *He's single*, one said. *No, I heard that he's engaged to some woman, and he's still got another girlfriend! Just like his brother—a playboy.*

His favorite overheard tidbit was he was a tremendously generous lover, which per the chatter, at least two of the ladies in the outer office area would be both willing and glad to offer their services to confirm. *Gee. How helpful.*

He's a millionaire, like Devin, another whispered.

Declan rolled his eyes. Not quite.

Declan decided enough was enough. He sighed, pushed his chair away from his desk, straightened his jacket and made to end the talk.

He strode out of the office, catching the women mid-sentence. One by one, the gossipers slowly quieted as they realized he was standing there, save one poor woman who continued to prattle on and on.

"Good morning, ladies."

Declan was amused to see that some of the women at least had the good grace to blush and stammer "Good morning, Mr. Hughes" the moment he came out of his office, knowing that their not-so-polite conversation had to have been overheard.

"Good morning, Sir. We didn't realize you had already come in for the day." The speaker was a smartly dressed young woman, a guilty look on her face.

Declan cleared his throat as he looked around at each of the women in turn. "Indeed."

Several women were studiously looking down at papers in their hand and attempted to back themselves into cubicles, trying for nonchalance. Declan was not fooled.

"I won't keep you from your work, as I'm sure you all have plenty to do today; but which one of you has been assigned to work on my requests this month?" His brother Devin had assured him that he would have whatever office and clerical help needed while working in the Whitfield office.

All the eyes in the room moved over to the organized but empty desk of Pam Jenkins.

"That would be Pam, Mr. Hughes. Pam Jenkins has been, like, assigned to whatever you need for, like, however long you need." The young woman reddened and snapped her gum, looking away.

Declan overheard the disappointed why not me sighs of the two women closest to him. Other than that, it seemed like everyone else was frozen in place, incapable of speech, incapable of movement.

Declan knew his staff had very little accurate information about him, especially in an office where he rarely made an appearance. Although the gossip was a touch uncomfortable, to Declan and his brother it had become second nature to keep private matters private. Their father had been adamant about that.

The discomfort of those caught gossiping; however, was hanging in the office like a cloud. Declan decided he could relieve that.

"And where is Pam on this fine morning?" He asked, jovial and overloud.

"She arrives every morning at 8:30, sir."

As if on cue, the elevator door opened. Through the glass office doors Declan and all ten of the office staff watched the older woman plod out of the elevator, smooth down her skirt and march into the office.

At least 70 years old, Pam reminded Declan of a charging bull. A charging bull wearing black orthopedic shoes.

Her eyes narrowed as she spied all of them watching her approach through the glass doors.

Declan sighed, then smiled. So this was Pam. *Well played, brother.* Leave it to Devin to pick not just the most *sensible*-looking woman in the office to help him out but the one from his first impression, who would be the most immune to his charm. He chuckled.

"Good morning, ladies." Pam walked through the door, her eyebrow raised as she looked around at her staff. Declan hadn't seen an eyebrow go up that high since Sister Mary Pat caught him with his hand on Rose Lucas's rear at the seventh grade dance.

"It IS time to get your day started, ladies, is it not?" Pam asked as she plunked her handbag and brown bagged lunch on the desk. "Are we having some sort of meeting?"

Obviously terrified of Pam, the red-faced women scattered to their desks. Immediately, the sounds of typing and phone calls being made filled the air.

"Mr. Hughes. Sir. Good morning. I'm Pam Jenkins. Your brother has informed me that I'll be assisting you with whatever you need."

"Very nice to meet you, Pam." Declan held out his hand shake hers, but Pam turned at the last second so that he was forced instead to take off her jacket with his proffered hand.

He had seen this very jacket on his grandmother, probably 40 years ago. Pam patted her helmet of gray hair and looked expectantly at Declan. The woman meant business.

Declan was flummoxed. Forces of nature had nothing on her.

"Yes, well, *right* then. As you know, I will be working on the Whitfield Hospital project, so I'll need all of the files we have on it…even things you think might be related. Keep your eyes open for the ecology studies on that area and bring those in too, if you would."

She even nodded efficiently, he thought, bemused.

Declan pondered another moment.

"I have some questions about some of the concerns of the Whitfield citizens; I'll need a list compiled of their questions for when I meet with the city planner. So, come on back and see me when you're ready."

Pam was nodding and took notes with a pencil that suddenly appeared from somewhere deep in her steel gray bouffant hairdo. *Where had that been hiding?*

"That's all I can think of for the present. Devin said he would be sending the minutes from our last village board meeting for me to review, so I'll need to see them as well when they're messengered in.

"Oh, and Pam, can you see if you can make a better pot of coffee and bring me a cup?" *For the love of all that's holy?* "I did my best this morning when I came in but it probably isn't as good as yours." He turned to walk back into his office. "Cream, no sugar. Thanks."

He slowed as soon as he realized that the office had once again gone silent—no clicks on the keyboards, no chatter on the phone.

He turned back to face Pam, who was standing now with her formidable arms crossed, head tilted slightly to the side and, so help him, the toe of her sensible shoe tapping. She paused dramatically before speaking.

"Mr. Hughes. Of course, I will immediately begin to gather any information that you need, sir, and I will be glad to bring that on in when it gets here." She made quotation marks with her pudgy fingers.

"But, Mr. Hughes, let's get one thing straight. I am *not* your coffee girl. Our staff is not going to be fetching your coffee, either." A few of the women looked disappointed

"I will, however, be glad to show you how to make a decent pot of coffee." She ended her statement with a firm nod and clumped back to her desk. "Just let me know when you'd like a coffee making lesson. Ladies, ladies, back to work."

Declan blinked. *What just happened?* Did he just get *schooled* by the office manager?

Declan threw his head back and began to laugh. Of course. He could see why this steel gray battleship was the one who ran this office. One look at that raised left eyebrow and those administrative assistants would stay on task. Every office needed a Pam.

His easy laugh seemed to relax the staff back to work. Here was womankind, once again, teaching him a lesson, he thought.

His smile faltered as he saw the old, framed pictures of his family on his office wall. How had it come to this? His father's death a few months ago had affected him. It had been a heart attack. His father's doctor, trying to be kind, told the family, "These things happen." *Not to my dad. Not to someone as healthy as he was.*

Their family had sat unbelieving in the emergency room. "Heart attacks happen, regardless of how healthy someone seems." the doctor continued, as if reading Declan's mind. All he could think was that if he had been here when it happened, things might have been different. Maybe help would have arrived sooner. Maybe the day would have gone differently. Maybe.

It was what brought him back to Whitfield. The brothers and their father had run the main office of Hughes and Sons in Illinois for years, and recently Declan had been in Portland opening up a smaller branch facility of Hughes and Sons. Devin had asked Declan to fly in and help him as jobs were starting to pile up after their father's death. He would be leaving town for a few weeks scoping out job sites and needed Declan to work out of the Whitfield office.

Pam broke his reverie with a sharp knock at the door. "I have those documents you were looking for, Mr. Hughes. I could not find much on the latest village board meetings regarding the project and the standstill we're at, however. I'm not sure if the other Mr. Hughes hasn't sent them, or if we just never received them. The books we procured on the history of our town are still in Mr. Hughes' possession as well." *Dammit. Why wouldn't he have left them here? Par for the course, Devin, par for the course.*

She placed the pages on his desk, straightened them and patted them. "If you'd like, I could send one of the staff to the library to pick up additional books? I've called ahead and asked them to place them on the side for you."

He had grabbed the pile and was sorting through them as he listened to Pam talk. At the mention of the library, he stilled. *Her.*

Grabbing his coat, Declan shook his head at Pam. "Thanks, but you know, I think I will do that errand myself, Pam. It will be good for me to get a feel of the town again, even though it hasn't been all that long since I was here. And get a breath of fresh air, too. I've been sitting here a while." *And some coffee. Some good, strong coffee.*

"Very good, then. Pam excused herself.

The library. Her hair. Her. Damn straight he knew where the library was. More intriguing was the young lady who was working there.

Baylyn Travers. He hadn't stopped thinking of her since he saw her.

Chapter 3

Thirteen years earlier...

Finally, *finally*, Brian Foster had noticed her at school. It didn't seem to bother him that she wore braces; that she was all awkward, long, gawky limbs. She had been hoping beyond all hope that he might ask her to the Homecoming dance being held at her high school.

After being virtually ignored by boys, having the object of her heart's desire stop her in the freshman hallway and stammer out an invitation to her in that deep voice of his was epic. Epic!

Taking the unspoken cue from her friends to act cool, she promised him a note by the end of the school day with her decision, although if he couldn't tell her answer was yes by her shining blue eyes he didn't deserve her anyway.

By homeroom, their final class of the day, she passed back a note via four other students that said, simply, yes.

As Baylyn's face burned with embarrassment, every single person giggled as they read it on its way to the back of the room where Brian sat. Perhaps the note hadn't been such a good idea.

It didn't matter. Brian was taking her to the Homecoming dance. He was lanky, also had braces and brown eyes and a shy smile that made Baylyn's heart sing. He also had a shock of dark hair that he always shoved back with his hand. She especially loved the fact that he wore Polo cologne. It was so sophisticated. No one else existed for her.

Elise didn't think the talk she needed to have with Baylyn would come so soon. Oh, it wasn't *that* talk. She had that talk with her daughter a few years ago. Elise had preferred that Baylyn would be interested in someone in her witchcraft education class, (mostly herbs and healing) or maybe even in her "Coven's Oven" cooking class.

Yes, she had hoped that *this* talk…the one about who is appropriate to date…whom she *had* to date…would wait for another day.

Life, however, just wasn't that simple.

Blessed with the gift of sight, Elise had hoped that she would see this coming, but that wasn't the case. Magic was funny that way.

On what was a perfectly ordinary day in September, the day she made those marvelous blueberry muffins with "quicken" in them (for love spells) her daughter had floated home on a cloud, stars in her eyes, to tell her mother that Brian Foster had noticed her. Actually talked to her. *Actually asked* her to the Homecoming dance with him. Maybe even *liked* her.

And apparently she had floated home on an *actual* cloud, judging by the condition of her brand new school shoes, the toes of which were all scuffed as if she were dragged home. As Baylyn hovered into the house, Elise took advantage of her daughter's distraction to push Baylyn's shoulders down gently, under the guise of a big hug, so that her feet actually touched the ground. Elise sighed, even as her heart lifted to see her daughter so happy.

"You know, you shouldn't be using your powers out there in the open. It's showing off, Baylyn. I won't have it. You need to be more careful." Elise said.

I should never have taught her that damn spell.

"Momma, he asked me to go to the dance with him!" Baylyn twirled her way over to a snack bar stool and settled into it as her mother took a batch of muffins out of the oven. They smelled divine. Reaching for one, she quickly pulled back, eyeing her mother suspiciously.

"Did you put something weird in these? Sometimes your muffins taste weird."

Elise looked sheepish. "*Yours* are still in the oven, dear. Those…" she trailed off. "Well, I'm experimenting with some new ingredients. You wouldn't want these."

"Why, what did you put in these?"

Eye of newt and some hair clippings of the man her client paid her to entrap with a love spell, Elise thought.

Out loud, she said, "Different blueberries."

"And why shouldn't I float? PE class was *hard*, and I was *sore*, and I was thinking about Brian…I guess I just wasn't careful enough and I let a spell slip out, maybe. What's the big deal, anyway, Mom? Everyone thinks we're witches." *You'd freak if you knew I do it all the time,* Baylyn thought.

To her mother, she said, "I hardly ever do that, Mom."

Elise rolled her eyes. "I know you do it all the time, Baylyn." Elise looked at her sternly. At her surprised look, she continued, "My powers are up today, Baylyn. Heard everything loud and clear even thought you were talking to yourself. Better cloak your thoughts next time, darling."

Steering the conversation in another direction, she asked her daughter, "Is this that same Brian I heard you talk about before?" While she didn't want to encourage her daughter to like this boy any more than she apparently already did, Elise was loathe to burst Baylyn's bubble of happiness.

Surely this one dance couldn't hurt anything. Family dictates discouraged against marrying someone outside of magic, not dating outside of magic. It paid to not play with fire and only look within your known circle of witches for a possible husband. However, there were no rules against dating outside of magic. *Just don't get too serious.*

Thankfully, Elise had found someone who was appropriate—Charles—and married him. They were happy together until his disappearance.

For Baylyn's father, Elise's greatest love and the father of her unborn child had disappeared. Simply disappeared. No one knew where he went, what spell might have been muttered and who muttered it. He simply winked out of existence, as if he had never been there.

She was heartbroken. Their love had been pure and true. Her grief over his death was such that during that same year, although the trees in the area were able to bud, they did not produce leaves. Nothing grew. Gardens failed as if in a draught. Mother Earth herself mourned along with Elise. Flowers grew only to wilt despite sunshine and water from desperate gardeners. During the hot sunny summer, although they received adequate rain, farmers' crops died in the field, no matter how hard they tried to keep them alive.

Baylyn's happy voice bubbled over her, bringing her back to the present. "Oh my gosh, mom, he's so cute! He just...he just...oh my *gosh*! I have to call Cat!"

She eagerly leaned forward to kiss her mother on the cheek and squeeze her excitedly. "EEEEE!" she squealed, then jumped up in the air, turned, and ran to her room.

"Floor, Baylyn." Elise reminded her without looking; sensing Baylyn was once again using that dratted floating spell.

Elise would have given anything at that moment not to have the sight. Even as Baylyn half walked, half floated up the stairs, Elise could see in her mind's eye what would happen at the dance Bay was so excited to go to. How that little snot Brian had taken a dare to ask Bay, the witch's daughter to the dance. How he had asked her only so that she could "conjure" up something extra to put in the punch. How he and some of his already tipsy friends had taunted her when she refused, saying she wasn't a "real" witch, because otherwise she'd prove it.

How Baylyn would spend two whole days in her room crying while Elise tried to comfort her. "Sometimes boys use girls, Baylyn. Especially girls like you, who have a special gift. Be careful who you trust, Baylyn, or you could be hurt again."

Elise shook her head as she took the regular muffins out of the oven. Baylyn had magic, all right. She was going to be a very powerful witch if she could already work a floating spell and not even consciously do it at the age of 17.

If she keeps progressing at this rate, I cannot even fathom how powerful she'll be when she turns 30 and the full measure of her power is realized.

Chapter 4

"I have her." Cat whispered.
"You do? For how long?"
"Long enough. Are you interested?"
"Oh yeah. Where you at?"
"Park. Twenty minutes?"
"I'll be there. Don't let her fall asleep." They were both smiling as they hung up.

Cat spotted Baylyn right away and puffed up with pride as Baylyn headed her way.

"Where is she?"

Cat angled the stroller carefully so as not to get sun in her niece's eyes, then pulled the light blanket down just a bit so that Baylyn could see Cat's precious two month old niece, on loan from one very tired and grateful sister.

"Oh, my gosh. Have you ever, I mean ever…"

"Right? Couldn't you just eat her up?"

"Of course she fell asleep. Sorry, Auntie Baylyn. No cuddle duty required. You want to walk a bit with me?"

It was a beautiful day, a little cloudy from time to time, but not chilly enough to keep the baby inside. The two women meandered around the park on the beautiful bike path that surrounded a picturesque little fishing lake. Cat was the most wonderful aunt and simply glowed when was talking about her only niece.

They could hear the joyous bark of a big black lab that was busy fetching a tennis ball out of the water when his owner threw it.

Across from where Baylyn and Cat strolled, there were families fishing as well as a couple of lone fishermen, drinking coffee from the local gas station and trying to land the big one. They settled in on a bench in the dappled sun.

The soft wind moved through the trees in the park with a sibilant hiss. Bay's gaze settled on the willow tree to their right, remembering the day her mother taught her how to choose a wand.

This is a willow tree, Bay, and this is one of the best types of wood for your first wand. It has a wonderful feminine energy. We must not just take a branch, though. You must first ask permission of the tree."

A six year old Baylyn looked up at her mother. "How do I do that?"

"You have to give the tree a big warm hug and ask for the wand meant for you."

Baylyn wrapped little arms around the scratchy tree trunk and said in her clear musical voice, "Can I have my wand? Pretty please." Her mother nodded approvingly.

She stepped back from the tree. "Now what, Momma?"

"Now we wait, darling." With the next gentle breeze, a pointed stick perfect for a wand dropped obediently to the ground at Baylyn's feet. Elise clapped her hands delightedly.

"Wonderful! Take good care of it, Baylyn, because it was a gift from the Goddess."

Baylyn smiled with the memory while Cat slowly pushed the stroller back and forth with her bejeweled ballet flat.

Wistful, Cat spoke. "I can't wait to have babies. Look at her. So cute."

"Speaking of cute, love your flats. Not your usual style."

"Just switching up a bit." Cat held out a foot and rotated a playful ankle. "Actually, I'm just stretching them out for my sister." She straightened the baby blanket, cooing at the baby. The love she had for the child clearly radiated through.

"Cat, if you ever want a family, you have to lower your standards for a man just a little bit."

"Look who's talking—the Queen of First Date Kingdom."

An athletic group of teens appeared to be starting up a football game in the far turn of the bike path around the lake, in the open field. The faint sounds of yelling joined the quiet exclamations and laughter of the families in front of them. People had waited a long time for summer and they were out in droves, enjoying the weather.

"Hardly fair. You know why I haven't dated a lot lately. How does it go? Cheat on me once? Shame on you. Tell me you're sorry, it will never happen again, only to find out it had been happening for six months and I was being dumped for her? Shame on me. For being an idiot." Baylyn shook her head slowly. It wasn't just a chapter in her life. Four years she had spent with Rob, who she had thought to be the man of her dreams.

"I've got major trust issues, Cat. Working on them, of course, but it's just harder for me to take that leap." The pain of that time wasn't near as fresh but stung a bit nonetheless. "Plus, my last few dates have had, well, one problem or another."

Cat nodded and touched Baylyn's hand. It had been a very difficult time for her best friend, but Cat was ready to see her friend brimming with the excitement of dates and romance again. "Have you thought about one of the e-dating sites yet?"

"No, probably because there's nowhere to write in oh, PS, be patient with me since I dated a serious jackass and still have some residual issues." Baylyn laughed and sighed at the same time. "This is the 21st century. Maybe we should try speed dating."

Cat snorted out loud. "Wait, no way!" She pointed at Baylyn and started laughing. "I've watched you when you think someone is cute. I bet if we went on a speed date, you'd be so nervous you'd barely get one sentence out before it would be time to switch!"

"Oh, stop, you." Baylyn left out the fact that she actually tried one of the online dating sites. Using a free seven day trial, she signed up with a picture for one weekend, felt foolish, took her profile and picture down, and never went back to that site again. She hadn't even had any dates resulting from that site.

Well, not exactly, she corrected herself. There were a couple of men who responded to her profile but suggested activities she wouldn't engage in on the first date. Or ever.

They both stood up and stretched a little, resuming their stroll through the park. The breeze had died down a little and the temperature was warming up. Baylyn adjusted the cover on the stroller.

"Cat, why aren't you on that matchup service? Or any of them?"

"Really?" Cat stopped to stroke the baby's lips with the pacifier until she took it back, her little cries stopping. "You know my requirements. Nothing less will do."

"Remind me again."

Cat sighed in frustration. "I think you just want to hear me talking about men so it takes the attention off of you and I don't forget the species exists."

Baylyn kept on her. "Dark hair? Light hair?" She prompted.

After rolling her eyes, Cat began. "Dark blonde hair. Wavy, not curly. Has to be clean shaven. Not too tall. Not a musclehead. Blue eyes."

"Cat, you're describing a Ken doll."

This time, Cat ignored Baylyn. "And his wild oats better be sown already. I'm not looking to be someone's mama, scolding him because he stayed out too late with all of his friends." She thought some more. "Sophisticated. Knows wine. White collar job." She smoothed her hair and wouldn't look at Baylyn.

Baylyn leaned closer to her friend and looped her arm through her friends', mindful of her stroller pushing, and gave her a squeeze. "So, the opposite of everything Bud was."

Cat shot her a dark look.

"You can't paint all guys with the same brush. There are wonderful men out there. The right one will treat you like a queen."

"Speaking of wonderful men…" Baylyn noticed they had walked almost all the way around the park and was surprised to see they had been talking more than watching the scenery. Directly up ahead was a group of men who had decided to play a pick-up game of basketball.

There were eight men, various ages and shapes, playing a boisterous game of shirts and skins. To Baylyn it looked like a lot of fun. Everything a guy could want, she mused, as she watched the lot of them jump athletically into the air, landing on each other almost as much as the pavement. *Like a pile of puppies.*

The sun was still out, keeping the "skins" team comfortable but judging from the copious amounts of sweat she could see glistening on backs and chests…

Baylyn gulped. "Oh, my God, that's him." she muttered under her breath. She flushed and went cold at the same time. She tried for a breezy tone as she said, "Oh, let's just turn around and go back the other way. I don't want to go this way." Baylyn went for cheerful and oblivious, but she knew Cat wasn't fooled for a minute.

"Who's over there that you want to avoid? Shirts or skins? Hmm....let's see here..." Obviously she was taking great pains to study each man, much to Baylyn's dismay.

"Oh. Oooh! That's him, isn't it? The library guy?" Cat waved toward the group.

"What are you doing?" Baylyn hissed. She grabbed Cat's hand and pulled it back down. "Seriously! Stop. I don't want to talk to anyone today."

"I wouldn't want to say hi either, looking like that." A confused look came over Cat's face. "Just kidding. I wonder where that came from. Sorry!"

Probably for the best. Besides, I wouldn't be able to hear him over my own heartbeat. Lord, that man's handsome. Places too long dormant on a healthy woman began to wake up and clamor for attention. Cat and Baylyn slowly pushed the stroller through the grass toward the cars, their only other option besides turning around completely and walking the 45 minutes in the other direction.

His chest. His stomach. Her breathing sped up. They passed close enough that Baylyn could make out shoulders that went from here to here. *That doesn't just occur in nature,* she thought. *Far too perfect.*

"Oh, good Lord." Baylyn fanned herself. "Hand me my water bottle, would you? I suddenly need something to drink."

Chapter 5

26 years earlier

"I'll take another." Reynaud Puckett said, gesturing vaguely at the small table where he was breakfasting.

"Another what, sir?" said the young waitress, confused. She was brand new and clearly she was frightened of him. She should have been because God, she was incompetent. Her interactions with him had not gone well up to this point. Reynaud did not like women who didn't know exactly what he wanted, when he wanted it.

This waitress, of course, had failed him miserably, as he knew she would. She dripped hot coffee on his hand, forgot the butter, and dropped his muffin. To reward her for her stellar service, he called her stupid and would have loved to have landed a swift kick on her backside, had she not been quicker walking away. More's the pity.

He turned strange black eyes her way and spoke so softly she could barely hear him. "Another coffee, you nitwit. And if you spill a drop, I will see to it that you are immediately relieved of your pitiful responsibilities here. Do we understand each other?"

Miserable and red faced, the waitress nodded. "Right away."

It was very fortunate that he had picked this particular establishment for his morning meal, he thought, as the timid waitress managed to refill his cup successfully. Aside from the incompetence of his waitress, he was delighted the table where he was sitting afforded him an unhindered view of the family owned shop that sold soaps, lotions, and skin care items.

To those in the know, it *also* sold crystals, incense, pentagrams, special cloths for working spells, candles, divining rods and wands. They also sold special brooms. In this day and age, though, most witches preferred to go by car or bus. How did the joke go? No splinters and it got you there faster. He enjoyed keeping an eye on the comings and goings of his fellow witches.

Taking a good long sip of his coffee, he caught movement out of the corner of his eye. Was that Elise? He leaned forward, eyes narrowed. Well, wasn't that interesting. He watched with no small amount of interest as the slender young widow ducked out of the little shop, magenta shawl pulled over her head against the November weather.

She looked around furtively around before she scurried down the street toward her car, holding a large wrapped package tight.

Although he was too far away from her to see her face, he could see her blue, blue eyes, little button nose, and the red curve of her lips in his mind's eye.

Elise. Damn. Could there be no one else who could stir him like that woman? As a member of her clan, he had vowed as all the other witches did to care and provide for her and the young Baylyn when her husband disappeared. Before she had ever married that weakling, Reynaud had his eye on her. He planned on making her *his* bride.

Some might have said that Charles was a solid, sturdy fellow, but Reynaud never saw that. How on earth a quiet, puny man like Charles could woo and win the dark-haired, seductive Elise was beyond him. Reynaud wondered sardonically how he even managed to carry her over the threshold with those feeble white arms.

Reynaud caught his own reflection now in the window. Staring back at him was what he thought was a fine-looking fellow. Dark brown hair pulled back carefully into a low ponytail. Brown eyes. Nose a little on the large side, but that was ok. So he had a little mole near his bottom lip. Added character. Without thinking, he lifted his ring finger up to smooth down his left eyebrow. Yes. *Dashing.*

Three years ago, Charles had disappeared under mysterious circumstances while Elise was still with child. She had had long enough to grieve, hadn't she? Wasn't it time to pick up the threads of your life and continue on, raising your daughter and perhaps including a new man in her life to call Daddy? Young children needed consistency, Reynaud reasoned. They needed keeping in line. As did their mothers.

He presented himself well enough to Elise, he thought. *I followed the rules…this time.* He sought permission from the council to court the lovely Elise, as well as care for her tiny daughter. One elder in particular seemed reluctant to bestow his blessing, until Reynaud reminded him that if he didn't want his wife to hear news of his enormous gambling debt, he'd do well to change his mind. Amazing how fast he changed his mind.

He sipped his coffee as he recalled what he referred to as their first "date", although others might not refer to it that way as it was conducted through her closed front door. He had gone to her house unannounced with flowers, intending merely to sit on her front porch with her. He'd take it slow, perhaps sip some lemonade that she would have ready, perhaps admire her smiling little daughter.

He knew that after three years, a woman would have needs. He wanted to be the first to fill them. He was everything she could ever need.

Instead, when he arrived, she refused to open the door. Through it, he could hear the sounds of pans crashing and her daughter throwing a temper tantrum. She finally peeked through the curtain at the window. Her face was flushed and a large spot of flour made itself at home on her nose. Leaving the flowers on the porch, he turned to go back to the car, thought better of it, and grabbed the flowers back. If the door had opened he would have given her the flowers. He'd just take them home and put them in water until he could get a normal date with Elise.

Although the door was opened to him on one occasion and he even got to come into the house, visits two and three did not go well. Baylyn eyed him with all the suspicion her three years could muster and Elise was uncomfortable and stiff with him, not even offering to make coffee for him, which would have afforded him at least the opportunity to watch the swing of her hips as she walked away.

Despite the fact that most people thought him a little thick, even he understood that this was not going to work. Judging by his whole three "dates", she obviously didn't know how to keep a house. Her coffee probably wasn't that good anyway. He couldn't really understand what her objection was to dating him. He was attractive. He had a good reputation, at least that she would know of. He had been willing to put up with her kid in order to claim Elise as his own, and finally be able to proudly parade around town as a couple. Her face would be turned up to his, adoring him.

Those dreams had been dashed. Now, it was more habit to pursue her than anything else.

Reynaud carefully blotted the corners of his mouth, contemplating Elise and her mysterious package. Everyone else coming out of that shop appeared casual, but not her. She was more furtive. He drummed his fingers on the table, deciding. Follow?

Yes, follow. She might not want anything to do with him romantically, but as the self-proclaimed watchdog to the council, he needed to keep an eye on the members to make sure they weren't up to anything nefarious. Some had practiced a darker craft within their clan. Why, he had an obligation to find out what she was up to. Whether she liked it or not.

Throwing his napkin down on the table, he peeled some bills off and tucked them under his plate; reconsidering at the last minute and pulling one back out to tuck back in his wallet. She didn't need a tip. As a matter of fact—he paused, blinking once, slowly.

Magic shimmered, like heat waves seen in the air. That should do it. The manager would surely find the cash register short, link it to the inept waitress, and someone else would be serving him next time. Hopefully more qualified.

The morning fog had burned off quite a bit, Reynaud found, as his long legs strode down the street on the way to Elise's house. Hard to imagine what she might be up to but he was going to find out.

The bundle was too small to be her daughter. Where was Elise's daughter? If not with Elise...his mouth tightened as he imagined another man bouncing the toddler on his knee, while Elise prepared a breakfast for them. His mind jumped from one scenario to another. Elise alone meant someone else was watching her child, which of course meant she was sleeping with someone else. His logic had never failed him before. His steps quickened as he thought of the possibility of catching her with someone else. Reporting back to the council.

Wait a moment. Did he want her to see him coming up the front walk? Shouldn't he take a much more circuitous route, maybe be able to come up on her and catch her in the act?

Abruptly he took a right on a side street. He knew the alleys and back ways for the neighborhood. She would never even know he was checking on her. A welfare check, he told himself. He was kind like that, always looking out for someone else.

Reynaud worked a simple cloaking spell in order to stay out of sight. He walked calmly, unhindered and unseen, but quietly up to Elise's door. He quashed a brief frisson of guilt for spying on her by reminding himself that it was for her own good.

Elise could feel his presence like a dark stain spreading on her favorite shirt, or a black cloud that blotted out the sun. She shuddered as she viewed Reynaud. Quickly thanking her neighbor for taking care of Baylyn, she ushered her out the side door.

Elise wasn't stupid; she knew that after three years single men of their council would be eyeing her with the possibility of marriage. They could try all they wanted, thought Elise. Charles was alive somewhere. Elise could feel it in her bones. She would wait for him and she would look for him. She would find him, too. She was as married now as when she took her vows to Charles four years ago.

She would find him, all right. She just needed the right way to look for him. She had limited success with scrying, and with so many places to look, and so many dimensions, there was no way that could be done accurately. Elise had sighed deeply as she used up her last hidden cash reserve and took the proceeds into town. She was going to find her husband using a crystal ball. She was sure of it. She only hoped that it would show her that vision first, and not the glimpses of inconsequential things that were going to happen in the neighborhood. Like the neighbor man four doors down, weeding the garden that wouldn't grow for another six months. A woman from across town humming while ironing a blouse she hadn't purchased yet. The 16 year old boy one town over washing the battered blue Subaru he would receive in three years as a graduation gift.

She concentrated on clearing her mind. What was making her uneasy? She got up, walked down the hall and quickly peeked in on her sleeping daughter. Seeing her daughter sleeping so peacefully did her heart good and gave her courage. Going back out into the parlor, she thought, perhaps she would start with something simple, like looking into the future and seeing who Baylyn would marry.

Elise carefully laid a round red tablecloth on the table. It was big enough to cover the table almost to the edges. She then sprinkled some grains of rice carefully on the flannel, and then centered the base for the crystal ball, then carefully; ever so carefully, the crystal ball itself.

The red flannel cloth had not only been embroidered delicately with powerful symbols and threads of gold but also enchanted so the scryer obtained a truthful reading opposed to a fanciful one that could be projected onto the ball. The spell also insured that only the rightful owner could use the crystal ball. She murmured the entire time.

It glowed an eerie, ethereal dark blue almost immediately. White mist rolled and muddled through the blue color, giving it the effect of clouds in a moonlit sky. Reynaud could see her slow smile of satisfaction.

Through ribbons of time, twenty years or more,
Reveal the true love my daughter waits for.

Nothing.

Still, she waited, yet the undulating fog just beneath the crystal orb's surface swirled lazily and revealed nothing. She tried again.

Through ribbons of time, twenty years or more
Reveal the face of the child I adore.

Immediately, the fog parted and there she was. Her daughter Baylyn, all grown up. *Oh, my.*

Elise flicked her fingers at the ball then directed the picture at the blank wall, enlarging the scene.

Unbidden, her hand rose to her lips. *My daughter will grow up to be a true beauty.* Her heart sang at the sight of her. As if watching a movie, she saw a montage, Baylyn's life as an adult and the very time she specified. She waved her hand as if turning pages in a book, briefly stopping when she saw one dark haired man but knew instinctively that was not him. Where was her true love?

As if fanning the pages of a book quickly, she peeked into Baylyn's love life.

And, nothing.

She had friends. She worked in what looked like a library. She seemed very happy but also resigned to the fact that the right one, her right one, would never appear. Impressions Elise got watching the screen were of betrayal. Insecurity. Mistrust. However, she couldn't identify what was causing those feelings.

Wait. She stilled. *What was that? Better yet, who?* She held up two fingers and centered the image between them, then opened her fingers, expanding the image as she did so.

Her breath caught. No. It couldn't be. Baylyn was still on the makeshift screen, obviously keeping fit by jogging, but the man running beside her?

Reynaud.

The same man who bothered her constantly.

The man in the image was without question Reynaud, but the face? It hadn't aged!

Impossible.

Her shock at seeing that despicable man having anything to do with Baylyn weakened her concentration, and Elise trembled as she scanned one image, then another, then another. There he was, at her library. The picture grew fainter. There he was, talking to her in a parking lot.

Too agitated to sit still, she wrung her hands and paced. She would never let that vile, repulsive man get close to her daughter.

Suddenly the skin on her neck prickled, a sure sign someone was watching her. She froze and wiped the image off the wall with a swift wave. Fear filled her heart. Her senses told her without doubt someone was near but when she reached out mentally, testing her immediate area for thoughts or impressions of her watcher, it came back dark.

Not blank.

Dark. Not dark, as in can't see, but *dark*, in that whatever was there had a malicious intent.

Carefully, as not to let on she suspected she was being observed; she wrapped the crystal ball in its flannel, all the while strengthening the protective spell around her home and specifically around her sleeping daughter. The rice grains rose up in the air and in their single file line dropped obediently into the cup set out for that purpose.

She made her way to her magic box and placed the ball within carefully despite her shaking hands.

I'll protect you, Baylyn. I'll do whatever it takes to keep you out of his clutches. He just wants power. Authority. Supremacy. For in aligning with Baylyn, daughter of a very powerful witch, he would sap most of her power and become far too potent. Elise needed to ensure that would never happen.

Reynaud too was shaking as he crept away from the house. Never had he seen such beauty. Never had the sight of a woman affected him the way that woman's image did. He knew instinctively that it was Elise's daughter Baylyn. Her beauty was stunning; her body, perfection. It was as if he had been punched in the solar plexus and was gasping for air.

He had to have her. He *would* have her.

His thoughts reeled. Here he was wasting his time on that…that…washed out woman Elise when all he needed to do was bide his time and wait for the *real* prize, her daughter. He thought greedily of the power she would bring to their marriage and once he married her, he would use it as he wished. She would be his.

Immediate gratification, however, tended to win out when it came to something Reynaud wanted. He didn't want to wait another 27 years for her. He wanted her now!

How to do it, how to do it. The wheels of his twisted brain spun and a dark smile spread over his features as a plan was born. Did he dare risk using the new spell he had worked so hard on? There had been little success among his peers for any type of time travel spell, save for Elise's perfect Charles. Perfect Charles worked on such a spell for a time, even was able to jump from place to place in his home, but never took the time travel aspect of it to completion.

After Charles's most permanent disappearance to date, Reynaud had been able to see the work in progress of his time travel spell, as all of his works were bought before the council. Despite his fear at being caught, Reynaud had appropriated Charles's work for his own use, copied it, and returned the original parchment. He refused to think of the punishment he would had suffered if he had been caught.

He continued walking slowly back to his home. Although Reynaud had finished the spell, he had never tested his time travel spell. What if it didn't work? What if he cut himself in half as he spoke the final word, with half of him being here and half being in the future or who knows where? Not only that, according to the notes meticulously kept, it only worked once. Only one try.

Baylyn's image swam up before his eyes, and any fear he had over giving it a try was erased. He had to try. Once married to her, their powers combined would make him the most powerful witch in the area, perhaps anywhere.

It was a perfect day, sunny and a little cool. In the park, Reynaud threw the ball again and again into the water for the wet, smelly dog to run and get. He wasn't doing it because he was such a pet lover but throwing the ball made a perfect cover for his plan to wander over to Baylyn and act surprised. "You're in the park too?" he'd say.

It was perfect.

He didn't need to stand too near her house to listen in on her phone conversations; however, it was a crapshoot on which ones he'd hear. Some were easier to hear than others. Listening in on her today, he knew Baylyn was going to be in the park for a walk with her little friend Cat and some baby.

He bided his time, letting them walk and get their chatter out before he made his move but just as he was ready to saunter up to her, he noticed that they stopped completely, staring at something in the distance.

His blood boiled. Of course. Of course he would be here. There he was, glistening with sweat, and Baylyn just stood there, panting over the testosterone disguised as Declan Hughes. Reynaud could sense she was getting ready to go talk to him and that, he couldn't allow. He hadn't come through the tunnels of time to be bested by a Neanderthal. He could easily get this "Declan" out of the way with a little well placed sabotage. Shake things up at work. Because if Declan was at work, he wasn't with Baylyn.

He found it hard to spell Baylyn, almost impossible, so he spelled Cat instead to place seeds of doubt in Baylyn's head about her appearance. You didn't get a chance to do your hair. Your makeup could use some retouching. You look like you are ten minutes out of your pajamas.

He watched the women walk toward the cars, taking comfort in the fact that even though he didn't get the chance to talk to Baylyn, neither did Declan.

Chapter 6

Baylyn blew sweaty bangs off of her forehead.

Baylyn had dozed on the couch last night, chilly, her new black kitten Theo snuggled into the covers up by her chin, her purr engine chugging away, and her paws kneading the blanket.

Well, it certainly wasn't cold today, thought Baylyn, as she pinned her black locks up in a clip. A few curls escaped and naturally curled here and there. The humidity was wreaking havoc on any style she tried. It always seemed the short little curls escaped.

She changed out of her work clothes, throwing on a pair of gray yoga pants, her running shoes, and a shirt that said "witches do it on a broom." After feeding her cat and doing a few stretches, Baylyn stepped out into the warm evening and began walking briskly. A few minutes later, she broke into a light jog and pulled her iPod out, set it for her running playlist, and put her headphones on.

About ten minutes into her run, she settled into a comfortable, easy rhythm, one she knew she could sustain for the entire hour. She then proceeded to check out. It was so automatic that once she was past her initial stiffness, she looked forward to almost every run.

Her breathing was deep and even and sometimes, like now, she felt she could run all night long, as if time was the only constraint and not sore legs.

So involved was she in her run that she failed to see another runner come up on her until he was right there. What was his name? He looked vaguely familiar. She mentally clicked through her library patrons. He had come into the library a while back looking for some information on a Whitfield property. He had been pretty demanding that Baylyn be the one to help him, but Cat had jumped in and taken care of him instead. She had described him as oily and annoying, and Baylyn had to agree.

Although he looked for all the world like he just happened to be out for a jog on the same road, at the same time, in the same place, from the looks of it his running attire was brand spanking new. Like he had just purchased it for this run tonight.

Baylyn's calm was interrupted. She could see him smiling and obviously he was yelling something at her. She very rarely saw another runner at this time of night on her path, especially a one that had proven to be a disruptive patron from the library.

She pushed her headphones down and slowed down her pace. "What?" *Hopefully he's just asking directions.*

"I said it's so weird that I run into you here! Crazy how that works!"

"Yeah." Baylyn gave him the side eye as he kept pace with her. "Weird."

Psycho. You probably figured out where and when I run and hid in the bushes til I happened to run by. It's how guys like you work. What do you really want?

"Nice night."

It was until you caught up with me. "Yes."

"Hot."

"Yes."

They began the semi-hilly trail up. Instead of her favorite running path to the park, Baylyn veered toward the heavily populated subdivision. Who knew what this whack-job was about?

She had already been running for half an hour before he had joined her on the trail, and was a little short of breath.

"I haven't seen you at the library the last few times I've gone." He wheezed his statement out and began to slow down. "I was hoping you could help me. I've got some questions that I hear only someone like you could help me with."

That stopped her in her tracks. Hands on hips, she faced him, breathing heavily. Narrowing her eyes, she asked, "There are many competent employees at our library. What do you mean, only someone like you?"

"Oh, I need things most people would consider fantasy." He motioned toward her witches t-shirt that clung sweatily to her body. "Making magic together." He seemed oblivious to Baylyn's discomfort and continued to stare at her, his eyes glancing every so often down to the strained logo on the front of her shirt.

"I don't even know you. You're interrupting my run. If there's something you need that deals with the library, you need to go to the library." Her hand moved down towards the pepper spray cleverly disguised as a pedometer clipped to the waistband of her pants.

"I have tried. You always seem too busy. I'm not sure why. I just wanted to ask you a few questions about something I've studied for a long, long time."

"What are you, some kind of reporter?"

"Of sorts." Reynaud put his hand out to shake hers. "Reynaud Puckett, at your service."

Baylyn glanced down and ignored his outstretched hand. "What paper do you write for? What kind of article?"

"I'm afraid I can't say on both counts."

Baylyn gave a little laugh of disbelief, turned on her heel, and broke into a light jog, heading directly toward Susan Jackson's house. Susan's husband was in the driveway washing his huge four wheeled drive truck. Bay would have help if she called for it.

As she did, she reached for her cell phone, making sure Reynaud saw her with phone in hand. She threw one more glance backward to make sure he wasn't following.

Reynaud hated to admit it, but the short distance he had jogged with her was more exercise than he had seen in months, years if truth be told. It was more than enough for him. The glamour he used only made him appear 20 pounds lighter. Inside, he was still woefully out of shape.

He collapsed on a bench in the park, watching her as she jogged easily away from him. Before rounding the corner of the path, she looked backward again. Spells, she was beautiful when she was fired up. He could tell she really wanted to stay and chat. Obviously she had taken his hint about the t shirt she was wearing. Why else would she look back at him? Obviously she was interested. She just must not want anyone at the library to know about their flirtation.

Message received, he thought, then smiled to himself. Yes, things were going good.

Shelving books was never the highlight of Baylyn's day, but with Cat's eager chatter about her percolating love life, it certainly made things a lot easier. Her animated demeanor put a smile on Baylyn's face.

"So, get this. I have this date with a guy that I've been chatting on line with for, I don't know, three weeks. He and I have, well, not a LOT in common, but we like the same types of movies and TV, he likes to bowl. Oh, and he actually was babysitting for his 3 year old niece when I talked to him once! He likes kids! He was so patient with her.

But get this, the guy, his name is Curt, he has this totally normal job of working in an accounting office. But guess what he does in his spare time?"

Baylyn opened her mouth to answer but Cat answered first.

"He is a paranormal investigator! Isn't that COOL???" She squealed.

Actually, that was pretty cool. "Are you kidding? Has he run into anything worth mentioning? Did he ever say?"

"Well, we met up for pizza and a beer. How normal, right? And he paid. And it was so calm and unhurried and I was hardly nervous at all, even though I hadn't met him before. And I told him, you just seem so normal! Almost…paranormal!" Cat giggled at her own bad joke.

Baylyn snickered. "Now that was fast thinking. But geez, Cat, I didn't even know you were talking to anyone on line!"

"I know. I wanted to see where it would lead first. After we talked about it in the park, I figured, what could it hurt? What do I have to lose?"

'That's the spirit. Tell me more."

"It's just very easy to be with him. It was one of the best first dates I have ever had. He was telling me about one of the cases he investigated in the neighborhood where he grew up. He said growing up as a kid there were always stories about this one house being haunted. And they actually got to investigate this same house. He told me that the EMF meters and stuff were going crazy, and they got some pictures of hazy stuff that they swear were like shapes or something. And that it was cold in certain places. He seemed to really believe there was something there."

Oh, Cat. If you only knew the kinds of "somethings" out there.

"Did you guys talk about going out again?"

"We have a date next Friday night. We're going bowling. And he has already called me twice since we went out. He's really sweet. But you know me, my defenses are up, and I really want to take this slow."

They chatted a bit about Baylyn's progress with the house, her naughty cat Theo and his fondness for socks, tissues, and toilet paper. Cat agreed that it was like having a little kid in the house but was glad to hear that Baylyn was enjoying her new kitten.

Talking and giggling with her friend, Baylyn could feel herself relaxing more and more. *This doesn't even feel like work. I'm so lucky.* She had felt unsettled for days and a few days ago cried Uncle, asking her mother, Elise, for some sort of charm to help her relax. She hadn't wanted to talk about the whole running incident to her mother—Elise was always so cautious about magic and people finding out they had it—so she was careful to cloak her thoughts prior to visiting.

"Mom?"

"Back here."

"What are you doing back there?" Her mother's house smelled so good, of cloves and wishes, cinnamon and magic. Baylyn found her in the three season room toward the back of the house, tending to her herbs; some were hanging upside down drying, some were newly planted and carefully tended, and some that were grown specifically for the more mundane use of cooking.

"I had a feeling you'd stop today." She crossed the room and reached out to touch Baylyn's cheek before stopping herself, laughing. *"I have half the garden on my hands right now. I made you some candles to take home. I thought you might like them. That should do the trick."* Ever the mother, though, she warned Bay to check with her if she had any questions about their use, or the order she needed to light them in.

"Mother, I think I can figure it out."

"Good, because I'd hate for something to happen like the egg spell."

"Gawd, why did you have to bring that up?"

Rob. *His name was Rob. And the trauma of their breakup was such that her mother, wanting to help her, told her of a spell that would help her get over their breakup. Baylyn would have tried anything at that point so following her instructions; she had stood in the bathroom, naked as the day she was born. She carefully broke an egg, then took the raw egg and rubbed it all over her body. When she was finished, she threw the egg shell in the garbage then spent the next hour showering, getting egg out of spots that should never see egg.*

Bay felt ridiculous the entire time she did it and to make matters worse, the spell didn't work. A week later she confided in her mother that the spell had failed. Her mother was puzzled and asked if she had followed the directions exactly and

Bay assured her that she had, and complained that it was hard to get all the egg off in the shower. How embarrassed she was when she found out that you weren't supposed to break the egg before rubbing it all over your body, but after, before you got rid of it. It took a while to live that one down.

That night Baylyn had carefully lit her mother's candles in the correct order, one in each room of the house. They smelled of white rose oil, sage, and sandalwood, but also her mother's house. Bay smiled as she felt her stress melt away. She didn't know if she was feeling at peace because of the spelled candles or the fact that they smelled like her mother's home had growing up.

"I can run the next two groups if you want, Baylyn. We've got a second grade field trip and a Me and Mommy group. You didn't even get to eat lunch yet, and you were telling me about all the paperwork you needed to get caught up on. Take your whole hour for a change, Bay. I got this."

Chapter 7

Knowing Cat was in the front of the library running interference so that she could finally get to her lunch, Baylyn felt like she could relax and enjoy her lunch break. There were still twenty minutes until the next big group of patrons came in. Tuesdays generally were very slow but not today; one of the clerks had called off from work and being busy helped the morning speed by.

Baylyn bit off another bite of her sandwich, closing her eyes in satisfaction. She was absolutely starving! The caffeine of morning coffee only gets you so far, even morning coffee like she made it, all doctored up with cream. There just hadn't been a good time to take a break.

Baylyn chewed slowly as she heard Cat's voice drawing closer to the kitchen. Her voice was accompanied by the low timbre of a man's voice.

"Excuse me. Hello?" Baylyn looked up, startled by the man's voice in the door and soft knock on the woodwork.

No. It couldn't be.

She set her sandwich down onto the wax paper, chewing her last bite as quickly as she possibly could. She slowly turned around, seeing Cat standing behind the gorgeous Declan. Cat was pointing at him behind his back, her eyebrows lifting up and down comically.

It had to be Tuna fish Tuesday.

There was a certain routine Baylyn followed. Might be boring, but that was how she liked it. Sunday nights she made meatloaf, so Monday's lunch was meatloaf sandwiches. Tuesday was tuna. Wednesday was Wendy's, Thursday was soup, (which didn't start with a "t" so Baylyn called it "thoop" privately) and Friday was French bread, fresh mozzarella and fruit.

Why, for once, couldn't her magic alert her to the fact that Declan would choose today to come in? And that further, he would come in at the exact time she had taken an enormous bite out of her sandwich? She could feel her face getting red and flushed and she dove for the napkin on the corner of the table.

Why couldn't he have come in on, say, a Friday? She pictured a lovely picnic lunch in her head. *Why, I seem to have more than enough here to share. Join me?* She would bat her eyes prettily, and then he would offer to get a convenient blanket out of his car to sit on. *Imagine, you coming along like this. How lucky! Here, have some grapes and cheese.* As if she were waiting just for him to show up, unannounced, for a lovely spontaneous picnic lunch in the park. And. AND. Friday was casual day so she would have had on a cute shirt, her new cute wedge sandals, and those faded jeans that did wonderful things for her backside.

As bad luck would have it, Declan showed up at approximately 11:14 a.m. Tuesday, after Baylyn had already lustily consumed half of a very oniony tuna fish sandwich on whole wheat bread.

On Tuesday, when she was gulping down her lunch because of a time crunch and well, it was Tuna Tuesday and Baylyn loved Tuna Tuesday.

She finally managed a smile at Declan. Where was her voice? Cat was mouthing "say SOMETHING" to her over his shoulder. She finally managed a greeting and stood to greet him at the door, smoothing down her skirt and hoping to lose any crumbs that had managed to land on her skirt.

"I'm so sorry to interrupt your lunch. I was here doing some research, and thought if you didn't mind...." His voice trailed off. He started again. "I happen to have my lunch as well." He wriggled a brown bag at her. "Would you..." he gestured vaguely..."care to take a walk in the park, tell me a little bit more about what's been going on in the area? Perhaps we can eat our lunches together."

Inwardly, she sighed. She had her hair pulled up into a sloppy bun, and oniony tuna breath; she had never felt less ready for potential romance in her entire life.

Even if it was just for a lunch walk in the park. Plus, why should she assume romance? Right now, she was just doing her civic duty. Helping a patron.

She nodded. Almost moving without her own volition, she was up and had gathered her lunch bag and was standing, ready to go with him. Traitor, she told her feet.

"Sure" she said weakly. Taking in a deep breath, she said it again, this time with more confidence. Looking at him, her stomach was doing warm, liquidy flip flops. She was physically unable to refuse him, though, not when he looked at her so those vivid blue eyes. Potential romance? Maybe. She would love that. He probably just really wanted to know about the area. She stood up a little straighter. Now if she could just tell her body to calm itself down, it would be fine. *No magic. No magic. No magic.*

It was no good. She still felt the telltale magic tingles going up and down her body that signaled a surge.

This was going to be a problem.

This was going to be fun, thought Declan. He admitted to himself that it was indeed an ambush on Baylyn—he had limited himself to polite but subtle flirty chatter and smiles the last few times he'd been there. She always looked so busy and preoccupied that he hated to disturb her any more by asking questions that were a complete front for just being able to talk to her—just to watch her eyes light up about a subject she was interested in.

He was spellbound the day he dropped in to the library during a story hour when she was reading to the children. To their delight, and his, she was acting out all of the parts, using different voices and she never sat down – instead, bending here and swooping there and making eye contact with each of the children, making the experience magical, entertaining, and yet personalized. The children screeched and laughed but listened raptly to her entire tale.

"I'll be back in a little bit, Cat." Baylyn said, as Declan opened the door for her and they stepped out into the bright, sunshiny day. On their way out, he pretended he didn't hear Cat whispering at her, *"He's so cute!!!!"*

"Where would you like to sit?" Declan asked, mindful of her skirt. He had already noticed a perfect picnic place he had scoped out a few days before.

"Any place is fine. It's so beautiful outside today, isn't it?" Baylyn asked, smiling up at him.

Her full smile caught him off guard. She was stunning. Her deep dark hair was clipped up, some pieces adorably falling around her face. He wanted to tuck one curl behind her earl. Her skin was so smooth. He appreciated her beauty, highlighted by make-up, but so natural looking. He was so done dating women who didn't even look like the same woman the morning after.

All that looking must have taken longer than he thought because she put a hand on his arm and gave him a look of concern. "Is everything ok?"

The shock of her touch went through her fingertips as she touched him, causing the hair on his arms to stand up. Her actual touch was electric, sending a bolt of pure energy up his arm, around his shoulder and down into his heart.

He smiled at her, unable to help himself. She was so damned cute. Those blue eyes, that long dark hair, that penchant for tweed...something about the whole package was making him feel like doing impulsive things, like sitting in the park with a business suit on during the week. He basked in the sight of her and drank in her scent.

He loved that she seemed to be a normal girl, with a normal appetite who enjoyed a tuna fish sandwich the way she did. Women who ate with gusto usually did everything with gusto, he had learned over the years. It showed a zest for life and all that it entailed.

Declan found the exact ornate curved bench he had seen earlier in the week for them to sit on. It was a gorgeous day, not too warm, not too cold, not too many bugs out to disturb them. There were geese everywhere, some lying on the grass and some chasing each other, while others made a tiny airborne trip to land in the small park pond and shake their tail feathers contentedly.

He opened the brown lunch bag he had with him. In it, he had carefully chosen foods that he could share very easily, should she choose to join him in the park. A bunch of red seedless grapes, small chunks of creamy Muenster cheese, and to wrap it all up, two thick chocolate brownies.

All right, clearly the man knew how to live. Any man who asked a woman to lunch only to ply her with cheese and brownies definitely had her vote. She wished she had a glass of wine, but her cold can of caffeine would have to do.

"This is such a surprise. I know you've been working on some projects lately for your company. How's that going?"

"It's going good. Really good. We have our little glitches here and there, but it's to be expected."

She changed the subject. "How long have you been back from Portland? Is it hard to readjust to a small town again?" *Holy hell, how could I have missed running into you anywhere?*

Declan smiled warmly at her. "Things like this sure make it a lot more fun."

Baylyn tried very hard to ignore the geese that were coming up behind Declan's chair. They seemed to be in some sort of formation. There had to be at least ten, marching two by two. *Bah Ram Ewe* Baylyn thought, working hard to fight a giggle. What WERE they doing? She tried to maintain her composure, fighting the urge to watch their peculiar neck movements and their synchronized movements, trying to keep her eyes on Declan's and give him her attention.

If she didn't know better, she'd think they were dancing. But that was impossible. She wasn't generating magic, was she?

Oh, my goodness. She was. She fought for control.

Looking at the birds, Baylyn really tried to pay attention to Declan. She really did. But when those geese started acting like the animated creatures in the insurance commercial, she found it hard to concentrate on anything but those damn things.

An old song about birds suddenly appearing played in her head. Had she been thinking that earlier while talking with Declan? It wouldn't be the first time her magic had affected her thoughts—producing catastrophic results.

It was a good thing he was facing her and wasn't able to watch the "dancing with the geese" production going on behind him. What would he even think, seeing a flock of Canadian geese shucking and jiving on the green carpet of lawn behind them?

She felt like wringing her hands in despair. Starting with a huge mouthful of sandwich, now this? Her magic flared up at the most unusual times.

This was definitely one of those times. Guys like Declan, guys who were the epitome of tall, dark and handsome (and smell so good) didn't just up and fall from the sky and into the tiny town of Whitfield.

The physical reaction she had to meeting him was something she had never experienced before. It had been so visceral. After their initial introductions, he had stayed well past closing time at the library, making small talk with Baylyn. It was so easy to talk with him while she tried to fix the copier. While they waited for the machine to warm up, they talked about their favorite authors.

When he had left the library that first day she met him, (when her library became a hotbed of magic gone awry) it was as if there was now an invisible silky cord tethering her midsection to his. She understood with a sudden flash of insight why women could wait for phone calls that never came. How they hoped to run into the object of their affection in the grocery store, the video store, the local fast food places. Why you would check your lipstick a hundred times a day, just in case you saw him.

All this went through Baylyn's head as she watched the chorus line of geese advancing troop like over to them, giving the occasional warning honk. He couldn't see this. She had to think of some way she could distract him. With him right in front of her, she couldn't counteract her own magic. She would need to think of some other way.

She could tell he noticed how her eyes kept darting behind him. She knew instinctively that to get him to keep his eyes on her, and hers on him and not on the geese, she had to start talking. That wasn't going to be much of a problem because when she was stressed…and this situation definitely was stressful…she began babbling.

Tearing her eyes off the geese and to him, she said the first thing that came into her head. Taking a deep breath, she began, "Do you like fall? I absolutely adore fall. I'm big into fall. Fall is my favorite season. The colors of the leaves turning those pretty oranges and reds—and, well, I guess not everyone has that reaction to the leaves falling, some people don't really like to rake, because then they're raking and bagging—but sometimes I like to just sit outside on the bench in my little back yard and drink a hot cup of tea—I put sugar in mine, do you?—or coffee, but I don't put sugar in my coffee—do you?—and just the other day a beautiful leaf wafted down and landed on my nose, because I had my head tilted back, and it stuck there, not because my nose is so big—and all I could think of at that second is how hot and sweet my tea was and how good that beautiful patchy orange and yellow leaf smelled and I was thinking, this is just a perfect moment."

She took a deep, much-needed breath and blinked her huge blue eyes at him. "Did you ever have a perfect moment like that?"

Baylyn paused. *Oh, I've scared him off. I babbled. Why did I babble? Why am I babbling now, in my own head? I do this every single time…get so wound up and nervous and bad things happen. My magic escapes and runs wild and scares the man away so fast that usually my first dates share the stage with the last date.*

Declan had been startled into attention when Baylyn began talking. He watched, entranced, as she tipped her head this way and that, depending on what she was saying. She gestured with her pretty soft hands from time to time to emphasize a point. She touched his arm for effect, which caused a slight electric shock. He watched her, bemused, and he drank all of her in during her little nervous speech. At the end, when she said, "Did you ever have a perfect moment like that?"—he thought to himself, *I'm having one right now, with you, here in this park, on this perfect day.*

"Go out with me." said Declan. She looked as if she didn't understand. He repeated himself. "Go out with me."

Baylyn slowly blinked her big blue eyes at Declan.

"What did you say?"

"Go out with me." He put a little emphasis on the word out.

Chapter 8

Inside, she was saying yes with all her being, until her common sense slapped her upside the head. Did she dare? Whereas she had finally opened her mind to dating, she wasn't sure she had finally opened her heart. This was the first time in a long time that she felt feelings for someone. All of the dates she had been on in the past had been awful. Disastrous, even. Why, there was the time she went out with Mitchell Browning. Nice guy. Handsome, with a shock of dark hair that fell beguilingly into his green eyes. He was a lawyer she ran into over and over in the produce section of the grocery store until one day, he asked her to go to dinner with him.

She hesitantly agreed. Although it was not exactly a rule, people of magic usually dated and married other people of magic. It certainly made things easier.

Anymore, witches were few and far between, and male witches were even rarer. So in order to have any sort of a social life—she had started—slowly at first, to date non magic men.

The night of their date, Mitchell Browning picked her up promptly at seven and had a beautiful bouquet of flowers for her.

This could be nice, Baylyn thought.

She was quiet in the car, listening to Mitchell talk about a particularly complicated personal injury case he was working on. Once at the restaurant, however, things rapidly went downhill as every single time Baylyn opened her mouth to speak, it was in a thick cockney accent.

Mitchell politely asked her to stop at one point finally, when she answered the waiter's question on whether or not she wanted something to drink with, "O'll 'ave water, guvnor!" The waiter, who was English, found her about as amusing as Mitchell did. Despite going to the washroom to try to sort herself out, all her words were too accented to repair the evening.

Face burning in embarrassment, she miserably nodded when he received a "call from his office" saying he was "needed on an urgent matter." The ride home was excruciating and loud in its silence.

Her favorite date, if you could call it that, was with a man whom she came into contact with during a college computer course. Calvin Alexander. Calvin was a writer and looked the part with a bit of a beard and brown eyes behind round glasses. Four weeks of what she thought was an unrequited crush culminated when Calvin turned around to talk to her and easily, confidently asked her if he could take her to dinner the following Friday.

She had gotten a pretty manicure and pedicure; painting both fingers and toes a purple mauve color and bought a new outfit. She left the salon with her hair trimmed and waxed everything that could be waxed. She and Calvin had several flirty phone calls and by the time he came for her on that Friday, she had major butterflies.

The butterflies were all but forgotten when they arrived at a tiny French bistro on the outskirts of town. This time, they were able to be seated and order a glass of pinot noir…and everything was fine! Baylyn began to relax and enjoy their conversation. Finally, maybe my tenth date is my lucky charm. *Maybe nothing is going to happen. Perhaps this is one date I get to really enjoy.* She looked deeply into his brown eyes. *Oh, I hope so.*

And that's when it began. It started as a tiny tickle in the back of her throat. She cleared it delicately and drank some water. She gave a tiny cough behind her napkin. Then another. Then it was as if she had been stricken with bronchitis as she just sat there. Calvin continued to prattle on about his project, completely unaware of her problem.

They ordered their entrees, choosing soup over salad. Eyes watering with her valiant effort to suppress her cough, Baylyn excused herself to visit the ladies room. He blinked owlishly behind his glasses, looking as if he were more concerned about how he would be able to remember where they were in the conversation when she returned than why she was coughing.

What is wrong with me? Why does this always happen? Is it me? It has to be me.

She powdered her nose and repaired her smudged eye makeup. It seemed the longer she was in the washroom the better she felt. *There. That should do it. I must have swallowed wrong or something. I don't even have a tickle anymore.*

She popped a cough drop into her mouth, questioning its age but thankful to find it despite its suspicious wrapper and fixed her lipstick, determined to actually complete one date. It wasn't so much the man any more…more the desire to see one damn date through to the conclusion. At this point she wasn't sure Calvin was even aware he was on a date so much as having his own personal sounding board.

She neared her table to sit down and could feel it coming upon her again. She sat down hastily and took a giant drink of water, trying to stave it off. Calvin looked very irritated; even asked her if she needed to go home but Baylyn swore through a runny nose and watery eyes that she was absolutely fine. *No way in hell am I giving in to this.* Calvin enjoyed books and writing almost as much as she did, he had a wonderful literary mind and seemed like such a funny guy. Couldn't she just have one normal date?

Their soup arrived and Baylyn lowered the napkin she had been holding to her mouth to muffle her coughs. She was hoping the warm soup would soothe away the coughing fit.

The moment the napkin lowered to her lap, however, a great coughing attack seized her. Through teary eyes, she watched in horror as the very cough drop she had been sucking on flew out of her mouth. It happened so fast she didn't even have time to react.

The cough drop took on a life of its own. Baylyn blinked frantically to see through her tears. It seemed to sail through the air leisurely, taking forever to land and when it did, it landed squarely in Calvin's soup with a cheerful little "plink", splashing up a perfect large drop of soup onto his shirt.

It was then Baylyn learned that you actually could slide from your chair onto the floor in embarrassment, even if it was a swanky restaurant, and why a seemingly great catch like Calvin remained single. When the soup landed on his pants he threw a temper tantrum worthy of a two year old girl, complete with tears, thrown napkins and loudly scooted chairs.

Later that evening, she sat watching a rerun of Golden Girls with a sub sandwich, her cat on her lap. She marveled with no small sense of irony the marked, miraculous recovery she had seemed to make the moment Calvin dropped her off at home and sped off.

No, her dating life had not gone well in the past. Wasn't it time for a change?

Shaking off the depressing cloak of her past dates, she decided to give Declan a chance. Perhaps her magic knew best of all. Short of dancing geese, she felt no accent, no itchy feet, and no coughing attacks.

Taking a peek at the bird burlesque behind him and the ten or so people who were now populating cyberspace with pictures and videos of a chorus line made up of geese, she pulled her gaze back to Declan's gorgeous ice blue eyes. She gazed at him for a moment before saying, "I would absolutely love to go on a date with you."

Behind him, the geese honked their approval.

Chapter 9

She hadn't been bowling in years. Baylyn nervously popped a mint in her mouth as she sat in her dark car in the parking lot, waiting for Declan. He was meeting her at the only bowling alley within three towns. How Cat had talked her into this double date was a mystery. Baylyn's last double date had ended in disaster, as whenever he neared Baylyn there was a terrible, noxious, sulfuric reaction in the air. Only a few things in this world smell like rotten eggs, and she was mortified to find out later that her judgmental date thought she was not very interesting and she probably should lay off the beans prior to date night.

Spectacular.

Punctuality was something Baylyn was proud of. She was early tonight, as usual, but surprised Cat wasn't there yet. She was usually as punctual as Baylyn. A text came through, startling her, and with a sinking feeling she glanced at her phone. Dammit, it was Cat and she was cancelling, as her sister had to work late in the ER. Cat and her date were going to watch her baby niece at the last second.

Now it was just her and Declan. Baylyn's pulse beat a bit faster. It was one thing to have a double date but quite another to be pitched headlong into a *regular* one on one date without any warning. She wasn't ready. *She wasn't ready.* She fingered the phone screen and toyed with the idea of cancelling just as Declan's truck rolled up. Baylyn took a few deep, deep breaths, her hand pressing on her midsection as if to quiet the butterflies threatening to take flight.

There was no turning back now.

She observed him as he sat in his truck, watched as he examined his teeth quickly in the visor mirror, and popped a mint or something in his mouth. *Points*, thought Baylyn. He leaned over to the passenger side, out of sight, and then unfolded himself from the truck; one Levi'd leg at a time, sliding into view from behind the door.

Oh, Lord, he was handsome.

He ran his hands along his belt, tucking his shirt into those nicely fitting blue jeans, and then smoothed his hair. Her magic was up. She could feel her energy coursing. Her radio began flipping channels erratically, startling her.

Declan leaned into the truck for what Baylyn thought was a jacket, but when he closed the door she saw it was a beautiful bouquet of flowers. *Oh!* She sighed. *Points, points, points.* The butterflies were encircling her heart now, and Baylyn put up a hand to quiet them. *Be careful,* her inner voice warned. *Sometimes things that are too good to be true ARE too good to be true.*

And sometimes what you see is what you get, so just shut the hell up, she fired back.

"I really am sorry," Baylyn apologized to Declan as they finished up the first game. Without four bowlers, they were relegated to a farther lane. Some of the league bowlers had finished, and minute by minute the bowling alley got more and more quiet. The next bowlers over were ten lanes away, so they were very much alone in their section of the bowling alley.

"Well, I'm not." Declan said, as he turned to Baylyn and smiled. *Oh, that smile.* He gestured to the scoreboard overhead. It was a sad representation. "That way no one else is witness to my humiliation. It's like I scored in binary code." She laughed as she realized his score was a series of 0s and 1s.

Bowling doubles had seemed like such a fun idea when Cat mentioned it…a few rounds of beers, some dreadful bowling alley cheese fries and fun with friends. A chance to watch Declan in a social situation, get Cat's take on him, maybe some flirting? The game was going much too quickly, seeing as it was just the two of them, with not much downtime between turns. Nowhere near as fun as it was supposed to be.

Bowling was definitely not a romantic sport. No, she thought, she should have had him take her to the batting cages. Have him show her how to hold the bat. Stand behind her and wrap his arms around hers….or wait…golf. Baylyn had never held a real golf club, just one of those from a miniature golf course. Now golf, that'd be perfect. She could honestly say she didn't know what she was doing. He would come behind her, snug himself up close, his hips to hers, his arms enveloping hers, his large calloused hands covering her more petite ones. He would need to lean down, of course, to tell her in her ear what to do. His hands would travel to her hips to move with his as she swung through. Maybe his mouth would move…

"Baylyn?" With a start, she watched Declan move his hand in front of her face a few times. "You there?"

A warm flush rose up her neck and pinked her cheeks. The tops of her ears, exposed from her casual ponytail, burned hot red.

She nervously licked her lips and stammered, "Oh, yes, of course. I'm so sorry. Just let my thoughts get away from me." Baylyn closed her eyes and pursed her lips and took in a deep breath. Upon opening them, she watched his eyes move from her flushed cheeks to her mouth, then back up again. She felt her heart give a slow, delicious twirl.

Declan unsettled her. She found it hard to believe that she was so drawn to a man she had only known for a short time. Yes, they had been talking for a few weeks on the phone. Yes, they had been texting, each one flirtier than the last. Her traitorous body was betraying her as well; wanting things she had no business wanting so soon.

She tried to collect herself, realizing when Declan was staring at her mouth that she was once again using her tongue to worry the one tooth the orthodontist never did get quite right.

Thank God his attention was drawn to her, because OH MY LANTA, behind his head his bowling ball was floating at eye level. She hadn't even realized her magic was trickling out. *But of course it is.* Hot guy on the brain…it was a wonder *all* the bowling balls weren't in the air.

"Drink," she stammered.

"What?"

"I would just *love* something to drink, wouldn't you?" She fanned herself vigorously hoping it would cover up the fact that she was muttering a tiny little *settle down* spell. Afraid fanning wasn't enough to distract him; she made a show of grabbing her purse and fussing to get out a $20, intentionally dropping her lipstick to keep his attention. He gallantly fetched the rolling tube, thus avoiding the hideous green 12 pound ball wobbling in a zig zag pattern in the air behind him *completely resisting her spell.*

"Dammit!" she said, under her breath, unable to take her gaze off the ball now—just praying it would drop before Declan saw. Quickly, she gave the spell a little *oomph*. The ball put up a good fight, but finally dropped down by degrees.

Declan, following her eyes, turned to look at whatever it was that had so completely captivated Baylyn's attention, just as the ball fell the last little half inch with a loud thunk.

Faint with relief, she shook her head. "Boy, those ball returns are *vicious* sometimes, aren't they? Good thing your fingers weren't in the way." She giggled, which sounded phony even to her ears.

Declan looked puzzled. "Yes, especially since neither one of us has thrown the ball lately for it to return anything." He cocked his head at her, obviously confused.

"Yes, well, about that drink..." She made to give him the $20 but he gently pushed her cash away, fingers grazing hers.

"Please. Put that away. I'll get it."

The ball began to make threatening sounds behind him. It had to be the contact between her fingers and his. Her magic was on the fritz. As usual, wonderful timing.

"I think something cold will do the trick." She moved her hand slowly away from his, tucking the money into her jean pocket. She fanned herself and a soft laugh escaped her lips.

"It was thirsty work throwing all my gutter balls. Takes real skill." She waggled her eyebrows comically at him.

Declan walked to the bar to get them some drinks. She knew if she didn't get her physical and emotional self in check, there would be more than floating balls to deal with. She cast a gentle *forgetting* spell on anyone who may have seen the floating ball. She had used the spell in the past on dates, having dealt with raining frogs, British accents; uncontrollable coughing and needing a way to help other people in the restaurant/theater/park forget what they saw.

He sauntered back with two cold beer bottles clinking in one hand and a basketful of popcorn in the other. *Yes! Points!*

"I figured I'd get something to snack on," Declan said as he settled the drinks and snacks on the table.

Truth be told, Declan was exhausted. The last few weeks he had been poring over his father's records and looking at a few of the jobs Devin had asked him to get started on. It was no wonder Devin had called him in. He was so tired at night it was all he could do to pull his boots off after walking his black lab, Dori. There was one thing that kept Declan going lately, though.

Baylyn.

He found himself thinking about her more and more often, quite a bit more than he normally would have at this stage of the game, truth be told. He thought about her at breakfast. He thought about her at lunchtime. He thought of reasons during the day to call or text her. Thoughts of her had finagled their way into his work day, which was definitely new for him. Surprising. Usually, Declan had no problem keeping his personal life from interfering with his work.

However, Baylyn definitely was different. There was something so pure, so amusing, and so enjoyable about her. She didn't seem to be in awe about his family financials. Declan prided himself on being able to spot a gold digger a mile away but Baylyn? She seemed to genuinely like being around him. Being gorgeous was just a bonus. He hadn't met anyone like her in a long, long time. He was very much looking forward to being with Baylyn tonight, and, quite honestly, thrilled her friend had canceled out.

Declan tapped her bottle with a "cheers" and took a long drink. Baylyn sipped her beer thoughtfully, yet still had that dazed look about her, causing him to wonder what she was thinking. Was it too much to hope it was thoughts of him that caused the flushed cheeks and shallow breaths? He popped some popcorn in his mouth and watched her for a few more seconds. On a whim, he tossed a piece of popcorn at her beer. It seemed to snap her out of it.

"Hey!" She laughed. She grabbed a handful of popcorn too and began munching it, throwing a few pieces his way. "Thanks for grabbing this. And for the beer. Sometimes there's nothing better than a cold beer."

There's a thought to warm man's heart, thought Declan.

"It's good that you enjoy it."

"It's my favorite kind, too. Of beer, that is." She leaned toward him and removed a piece of popcorn that had wedged between his buttons.

Before she could react, he grabbed her hand and drew the popcorn up to his mouth. His teeth grazed her fingers as he nibbled the popcorn. The short gasp told Declan exactly what he needed to know: Baylyn was feeling the same connection he was. Inside, he felt a surge of male pride; possessiveness. He pulled her fingers back to his lips and slowly kissed it.

"It's my favorite kind, too. Of popcorn eating, that is."

Chapter 10

"We're going to the bookstore!" Baylyn twirled around in her kitchen. Didn't hurt to have cushy socks on when one was in need of a serious spin.

"Theo! He called." *Twirltwirltwirl*.

Despite the fact they had talked and texted constantly, she was still excited when his number popped up. She had even assigned him a unique ring tone, a quacking duck, to remember their lunch in the park.

As if she could forget.

He had laughed when she suggested meeting at the bookstore.

"Believe it or not, that was my first choice of a place to go, but I didn't know if after being around books all the time you'd want to be around them on a weekend too."

But I'll be with you, she thought. Whole. Different. Ballgame.

She had always been a teeny bit jealous when going to the bookstore of all the other couples strolling about the library, steaming cup of coffee from the bookstore's coffee shop in their free hands, heads bent together to softly laugh and whisper. Now, much to her delight, she would be one of those people strolling with someone else. And it would be with Declan.

She parked her purple VW and found him easily as he was standing right inside the foyer of the bookstore.

"I don't know why you didn't let me pick you up."

Because I'm a little bit of a control freak.

"I have to stop and get cat food on her way home and didn't want to put you out." *True enough.*

He smiled warmly at her. It warmed her from the soles of her feet to the top of her head and certain places in between.

Oh, heavens. She was going to have to maintain control tonight so that there would be no floating inside the bookstore.

"I'm just really glad you wanted to shop with me."

"Are you kidding? You're combining two of my very favorite things…books and shopping."

And smelling that otherworldly cologne you wear. Good Ness. It's doing funny things to my stomach. So really, you're combining three things.

She adopted a playful tone. "So, what are the ages of the giftees?"

He chuckled. "Well, my niece Gracie is four and her mother, my sister Daphne, is 30. Again."

Baylyn looked at him over her spectacles. "Actually, this is a no brainer. Follow me."

She pulled the double doors open and the smell of new pages rolled out.

Declan caught her hand in his and laced his fingers with hers. Baylyn flushed with pleasure. She could feel her face reddening and cursed her fair skin for betraying her emotions. She casually peeked down at their entwined hands. His hand looked so strong, with long, tan fingers tipped by well-manicured, square nails. It felt so right, walking through the bookstore holding his big, warm hand.

I could get used to this. Breathless and giddy, she concentrated on keeping her feet on the ground.

This felt so right, thought Declan. The more he had thought about it, the more sure he was that the bookstore would be a fantastic place to go, not only because it was full of books and Baylyn obviously loved books, but because the atmosphere was casual, there was plenty to see, and lots of conversation starters. And coffee. He loved coffee, and he knew Baylyn did too. He figured they could each get a cup and wander around.

Casual. Laid back.

He felt anything but laid back at the moment, though. The feel of her hand in his, the way her thumb would gently caress the top of his hand—he didn't even think she was aware of what she was doing.

The little touches were driving him to distraction. What had he told her he needed? Oh, yes, some kind of diet book for his sister (her request, not his idea). His sister was the type of person who enjoyed trying different diet plans, always sure the next diet was the one that would help her shed her four year postpartum 20 pounds. Personally, Declan thought she looked absolutely fine the way she was, but he knew that would fall on deaf ears.

He decided she'd probably want the newest popular cookbook about eating meat on days that have an "n" in them. Or something like that.

Declan gave Baylyn's hand a little squeeze. "Do you want some coffee?"

Baylyn grinned. "Here, it's proper etiquette to stroll around with a cup in hand." Sotto voce, she told him, "in fact, I do believe it's actually a requirement."

Obviously no stranger to blends, she told the barista she'd like an iced tall sugar free caramel, nonfat, double shot on light ice. She turned expectantly to Declan.

"Regular coffee, please."

The barista looked at him dully. "Regular?"

"Just regular ol' coffee."

The two baristas behind the counter started smirking.

"Tall, grande, or venti?"

"No, just regular."

"No, sir, that's the size."

Baylyn convulsed in giggles. "Need help?" She turned to the girl behind the counter. "He'll take a Venti (at this, she emphasized the term and widened her eyes at Declan) blonde, with room."

It looked like Baylyn was valiantly trying to hold in her laughter, so Declan decided to play along, with a straight face.

"And hold the double…foo foo. And for the record, I prefer brunettes." He waggled his eyebrows at Bay.

They stopped at the sugar and creamer station and Declan added cream to his brew, then they ambled into the children's section. It was one of Baylyn's favorite sections—and she told him so. "Books. One of my favorite things. And bookstores. One of my favorite places." She inhaled deeply. "Just smell all those stories."

She took him in the classic book picture area to choose something for his niece, and then they wandered over to the popular newer titles for children. She spoke about the books, touching them, and retelling the story the way he imagined she would to an interested young library patron.

She has such passion, thought Declan. He noticed her animated joy as she spoke, the way her eyelashes fluttered and the crinkles next to her eyes when she came to a funny part. Her perfectly arched brows rose when she got to the good parts of the story. Her words barely registered as he focused on the way her mouth moved, the lilt in her voice as she told the story.

He was fascinated by the way she blew a puff of air upwards to blow away an errant black lock that kept drifting into her eyes. *Beautiful. She's so beautiful, and she doesn't even know it.*

They looked at books on humor and games, and when he wandered off to the history and archeology section, she meandered through the self-help section, noting various books on the magical arts. One in particular featured a mortar and pestle on the cover, and Baylyn remembered questioning her mother about their use when setting up her own household.

"Mom, how often do you use your mortar and pestle?" Bay had asked, gesturing at her mother's marble product sitting on the counter. "Would I use one often enough to need one?"

"Let me ask you a question, Bay. Do we use brooms to fly?" Her mother's eyes were sparkling as she gently teased her daughter.

Bay laughed. "No, Mother. But I could. I learned how in summer school when I got my 'other' learner's permit."

"Smarty pants. Yes, you could ride a broom, but a car gets you there faster. My point is dark roast beans aren't the only thing I grind in the coffee grinder. It's much easier, more thorough, to put your herbs in there. Plus, it's nice to take it all apart and throw it in the dishwasher on sanitize. You don't want traces of one spell contaminating the next."

"Mother, you are a veritable font of information."

She put the book down and after checking to see Declan was still in the archaeology section, she carefully sidled into the erotic book section. She was always looking to find something new to order for their sassy reclusive patron who seemed to have rather exotic tastes for her age. She was their best patron, after all. Most interesting, that's for sure.

Checking that Declan was engrossed in a book and unaware of what section she was in, she skimmed the titles. Here was one: "You Know You Want It, I'll Show You How." *Um, no.* Another, "Swings

Aren't Just for Children" seemed a little too...*too*. She finally settled on another and upon flipping through it, found that the writing was clear and intelligent, and the pictures left little to the imagination.

She held the book at an angle. Were these male or female legs in this picture? She couldn't tell. Goodness, didn't these people ever get a *cramp*? Her face warmed a little in embarrassment. As if sensing that, the book started fanning the pages for her, to try to cool her heated face. Her hair lifted and blew as the fanning grew a little more intense. Fumbling, she was finally able to snap the book shut, and she attempted to reshelf it.

The book resisted her, firmly planting both its front and back cover firmly on either side of its home on the shelf, and the spine of the book pressed backward against her hand.

"Oooooh!" she hissed. "You naughty little thing! Get in there before I..."

She realized she was whispering out loud around the same time she saw Declan peeking around the corner of the bookcase.

"Oh, there you are. Find anything..." He arched a brow. "Titillating?" He leaned languidly against the divider, enjoying her discomfort.

At that moment, the book decided to behave and slid obediently back into its place. Striving to be cool but unable to repress a grin, Baylyn blew into the sipping hole in the coffee lid. It made a loud whistling noise. So much for cool.

"Those pages were flipping so fast I thought it was one of those books with the tiny moving pictures. Hey, which one did you look at anyway? Let me check for those little pictures."

Baylyn suddenly realized they were face to face, both laughing, both a little breathless. He was so close to her. *Had eyes ever been so blue*, she wondered? Had any woman had a man look at her the way Declan was looking at her right now?

She felt both safe and hunted. She gave a tiny nervous laugh then bit her bottom lip. She became aware that his hand was up and over her shoulder where he was grabbing for the disobedient text, but that put him in very close proximity to her. *Very close*. She could feel his warm coffee scented breath on her, mixed with a scent that could only be described as a Declan-scent. She closed her eyes and breathed in deeply of it.

"Everything ok?" Declan inquired innocently. He leaned a little nearer to her.

She watched him come nearer and nearer still, until Declan finally closed the small distance between them by ducking his dark head and very gently, very lightly touching his lips to hers in the briefest of kisses.

Declan stayed to nibble gently at the lower lip. "You are even more delicious than I ever thought." he whispered, laying his forehead to hers. "I'm lost."

Suddenly a screaming toddler ran past them, interrupting the moment, grabbing onto Declan's pant legs for purchase as he raced down the aisle, followed by his father, who was yelling, "'Scuse me! Coming through!"

They broke apart with a smile. Declan gave her one final kiss. "To be continued, Baylyn," he promised.

Chapter 11

Sixteen tops. Twelve bottoms. Blouses and sweaters, ranging from sexy to prim. They all lay strewn on Baylyn's bed. Declan was due to pick her up in thirty minutes. She stood in her bra and panties, her newly painted wine colored toes flexing on the rug. Skirt, pants, blouse, sweater. Her toes tapped out the words.

Her last dates with Declan had been really lovely. Lovely, meaning he was a gentleman, but she could feel the dangerous, passionate undercurrent. It was delicious, whatever it was. They had spent the last date walking along the riverside, her arm tucked into his.

He was an amazing conversationalist and really listened when Baylyn expressed an opinion. His work was interesting; Baylyn enjoyed listening to all that went into his job. He made quite an effort to use the right terminology when asking Baylyn about her day and her patrons. She loved her job and being able to talk to someone about it was gratifying. They had picked up some drinks from one of the local shops and stopped to watch the ducks as the night turned dark. He tossed bits of leftover cookie to the ducks hanging around as they talked about their pasts.

She was getting better with controlling her magic when she was around him. It wasn't anything she had ever experienced. She tingled all over when he was around and her magic *was* heightened, but she was getting much better at getting ahead of it, especially being able to feel it starting to rebel. In the past, it felt as though her magic worked on its own to push away the men she had dated. For the first time, it seemed like her magic actually liked someone she was dating. It *liked* Declan.

Was such a thing possible?

Baylyn nervously thought about the fact that she had not told Declan, or even hinted, at the fact that she had magic powers. He didn't know. Was that a sneaky thing to do, or was she just being smart? Would he ever entertain the idea, or not even believe her in the first place?

Up until now, she'd tried to tell only told one other person—Rob—who used her at first like a magic rabbit's foot…predict this, buy a lottery card today, whip me up something. She balked at every turn, not willing to be used for that purpose until he believed her to have almost 'carnival' like powers. Not real powers. Not a real witch. And toward the end, he managed to make her feel like she was not even a real woman.

If only Cat had magic, she thought. *She'd understand.* Having a best friend without powers wasn't easy. There had been many, many times when Baylyn had almost confided in Cat but at the very last second, her mother's warning about telling people would ring in her ears, and she would stop.

Baylyn waved her hand over her bed. This gray silk blouse, black cardigan and red skirt? The clothing raised and formed a pose in the air above the bed. No, she thought, too boring. She pursed her lips and pointed her finger, causing all her clothes to dance about over her bed. Outfits formed and pirouetted as Baylyn started humming a soft tune. With a flick of her wrist, she started tossing the choices she didn't want into a pile. When one outfit remained, the decision was made.

She slid a sparkly plum colored camisole over her head, mindful of her soft waves and carefully pinned hair. Styled to look sexy yet casual, it still had taken her thirty minutes to pull off the 'just out of bed' look. She paired it with a short cardigan and an even shorter skirt, Baylyn was just buckling her t-strap high heel as the doorbell rang.

With the wave of both her hands, two claps and a few choice words, the clothes made their way back to the closet, her shoes stacked nearly onto the shoe racks, her bracelets stacked neatly on her wrist. She quickly checked her earring backs as she walked toward her door.

"Wow."

Declan's gaze told Baylyn everything she needed to know about her outfit choice. He enveloped her in a hug, and not for the first time Baylyn thought she'd be happy in his arms for as long as she could be there. He smelled amazing, and as she tucked her head right under his chin she moved her hands down on his arms.

He moved his hand up her back, slowly, sending shocks throughout her body. His warm hand came up to her neck, then brushed forward to her chin, then mouth. She tipped her head back to look at him just as his fingers brushed her lips as if marking the spot for his kiss.

The zap was sharp and quick, and the shock enough for Baylyn to pull away. "Ow!" She laughed, rubbing her lips. "Must be the static!"

Her lips still zinging, she reluctantly ended the embrace.

"Meet you out there."

She eyed his truck as she walked out. It was one of those off road style trucks, able to handle anything but still sparkling clean and shiny. It was lifted, a tall truck for a tall man. Baylyn's heel slid a little in the gravel. She looked down at her shoe, up to her skirt and then over at the truck before she noticed the running boards seemed very high. She couldn't help but feel like this wasn't going to be good.

Declan headed toward the driver's door instead of coming around to open the passenger door like Baylyn assumed he would. Well, fine. She walked over to the passenger side door, and decided that if he wasn't going to help her get in, she'd just help herself. With a touch of magic, of course, a little hovering up to the door height so she could daintily step into the truck. The decision made, she just needed to time it right so Declan didn't see anything. As soon as she thought she heard Declan's door open, she yanked hers open and fluttered her fingers.

Baylyn was in mid-rise, her lashes barely closed with slight concentration. She liked to think after years of practice she looked a bit like Mary Poppins as she lightly floated up to her destination.

The sound of boots on gravel alerted her to Declan's approach. *Holy crap.* She quickly put her foot out to catch the running board and her hands to catch the door frame.

"Whoa, here, let me get that for you." Declan said as he came behind her. He quickly put the bouquet of flowers under his arm to free his arms to help her. She had no idea he had been that close. She panicked a little as the toe of her shoe slid right off the board. Her grip hadn't quite made contact and her fingers grasped at the edge of the door frame. She squealed and several choice words flew out of her mouth as she felt herself falling, falling...

The rush of boots on gravel was all she heard; Declan was almost too late, catching her barely under the arms as she fell backwards out of the truck. He set her gently to rights.

It took her a minute, as she smoothed down her skirt and sweater to realize he Declan was barely suppressing a laugh. Indignant, maybe at being caught mid-magic, maybe because she had to have looked damned ungraceful, or maybe a little bit of both, Baylyn smoothed her hands down her skirt, a bit more roughly this time, and snapped out a "thanks".

The smile on Declan's face became wider. "It's just…It's just that. It's…" he choked out the words, finally giving in to the full laughter that had overtaken him.

Baylyn's face flushed red. "Oh, thanks. I could have really hurt myself just now and you are stuck with…" at this Baylyn mimicked Declan "it's just…it's just…it's just…" Her hands waved in the air, back and forth chest level as she copied what Declan was doing. She leaned over to pick up her purse and her wrap from the ground.

Declan began to wheeze his apology out. "I can honestly say, in all my years of being around job sites and men, I have never, and I truly mean never, heard language like that before." His hands now braced on his thighs as his laughter came back full force. "Especially from such a pretty little librarian." He barely got the words out before he began once again braying with laughter.

Baylyn looked at Declan laughing, her mind racing back through the last few moments. Spell, eyes closed, lifting, panic, whirling. *Oh.*

"Oh. My. Goodness." She said, her words looking and sounding dull in comparison to the colorful expletive words that had flown out of her mouth just moments before. Her blush deepened, Baylyn feeling the heat down into her bones. Her breath hitched and she thought she might cry of the embarrassment. That had to have been a thirty word sequence she yelled as she fell. She tucked her head down and tried to wish the embarrassment away.

"Baylyn." Declan stood in front of her.

He widened his stance and leaned in, bringing his tall frame down to her tinier one. He tipped her chin up so he could see her face. "Baylyn," he breathed her name. She finally looked up at him, looking first at his eyes, then at his long lashes, moving downward toward his lips.

"The combinations you came up with..." he started giggling again. Baylyn pushed him back a little bit and smacked his arm with her purse.

"OK! Enough! I have a dirty mouth, alright?" Baylyn primly tucked her purse under her arm. "You scared me, and I thought I was going to fall on my ass. And speaking of asses, by the way, you laugh like a donkey." She looked away, tapping a foot.

At the word "ass" Declan lost it again.

"Ok, what did it this time? Ass? Or donkey? What are you, 12?"

"What are *you*, a truck driver?"

Baylyn marched over to the truck door, putting her foot up into the cab of the truck. She hopped on her left foot, trying to grab the handle that was supposed to help you get in. She switched feet and tried hopping on the opposite foot. She had just barely grazed the handle when she felt Declan's warm hands on her waist, pulling her back down to the ground. "Easy, now," he said as she came up behind her.

Telling her she should hop when he lifted, Baylyn closed her eyes in embarrassment. Why couldn't he have a svelte sports car? Something super sexy, black, and *more importantly*, low to the ground? He began lifting her, it seemed effortlessly, and she gained a foothold into the cab.

His hands moved lower and felt hot through her skirt toward her leg as she settled into the cab. His hand followed the length of her skirt and paused. His laughter had slowly tapered off; Baylyn looked at him to see why.

His hand had completely stopped, too. His fingers were still on the skirt, but his thumb was roughly running back and forth between her skin and the lace top of her thigh high nylon. His touch was sizzling.

"Baylyn, I have never met anyone like you. I love that you're not afraid to be yourself around me," he said dragging his eyes to look straight at her. "Never have I had so much joy being around one person." He moved his hands up to cup her face and brought it down to his. He touched his lips slowly to hers and pulled away just as unhurriedly.

"I didn't mean to hurt your feelings laughing at you." He held his arms limp, his fingers tucked into the pockets of the front of his pants.

"You are so sweet, and sexy, and prim and your outburst, well, it just absolutely took me off guard."

Baylyn gazed down at Declan. It surprised her how quickly she had become irritated that he was laughing at her, but she realized that it was simply that she didn't want him to think badly of her. But really, it was funny.

"I'll try to keep my salty language to myself, sir," she said, pretending to fan herself. "Now, this here lady could use a drink and some dinner. Feed me, Declan, and all is forgiven."

"As milady wishes," Declan responded, sketching a bow, and then giving her a big wink before easing her door shut.

Reynaud was sitting in his car a block down, watching the entire scene unfold, incredulous. What was Declan doing here? Reynaud had taken great pains (and joy) to scramble Declan's paperwork to the point of no return, to make it impossible for Declan to be able to keep the date with Baylyn tonight. No way. And yet, impossibly, Baylyn was climbing into that ridiculous truck.

Reynaud had planned on strolling up to Baylyn's door, once Declan called to once again cancel their plans. Casually walk up to the door and maybe get Bay to go for a walk with him. Let her cry on his shoulder. Commiserate with her. Be there for her when it all fell apart.

Well this wasn't going to do. Not at all.

Chapter 12

I may have already had my last "first" date, Baylyn mused.

Sitting in the kitchen with a glass of red wine, Baylyn took the nail polish off her nails then clipped them down, humming as she did so. She smiled happily as she rummaged through her manicure box to find a nail file to smooth down the rough edges, and then slowly, dreamily, shaped her nails to her favorite length. It seemed like a lifetime since she had gone to the salon to have a manicure. *I've just been so busy lately. Busy with Declan.* Oh, boy, had she been busy. She grinned to herself.

Realizing she was 29 and not 16, Baylyn took pains not to think about the number of dates she had been on with Declan, preferring to instead concentrate on the relationship they had cultivated together. It seemed that all the first dates Bay had ever gone on with other men ended in complete disaster. Somehow, her magic had ensured that. But somehow, with Declan, her magic accepted him. Invited him in, she thought, remembering the day at the park when the geese trumpeted their acceptance.

Baylyn had finally come to the realization that somehow her magic had really done her a favor. By rejecting all of the suitors it knew were not right for her, magic was able to help her wait for the right man. Declan.

Despite all the talk about not counting dates, she knew they had passed the 20 date mark. Twenty dates. Twenty times that she had been with Declan for hours at a time, learning about him, his family, his views…and realizing how compatible they were in all aspects of their relationship. Never had she had so much fun with a man. Never had she thought so seriously about a future with someone. With Declan, she could picture it all.

He was funny. He was attentive. He was charming. He thought about her when he wasn't with her. He called sometimes during the day with something interesting to tell her, or to ask her opinion on something. Once he called when he was doing a crossword puzzle. He was waiting in his office for a package to be couriered over and needed a 5 letter word for jovial. She told him "jolly" and he tried very hard to make that work before calling her back and teasing her after he realized the word was "happy. You know, happy. Like you make me."

Sweet. Nerdy. She smiled at the memory and slowed in her filing. And those blue eyes, that dark hair, the way he moved and smelled and laughed and kissed. She had never been so physically attracted to any man, ever.

She was really letting her guard down with him, and it was so hard to do. She knew based on the wonderful time they were spending together that he was unlike anyone else she had ever dated. Baylyn felt hypocritical as more and more time passed and she had yet to tell him she was a witch.

Tell him tonight after the volleyball game, her inner witch admonished. *Can't keep this a secret for too much longer.*

Bay held her unpolished but manicured hands out in front of her with a critical eye, checking her handiwork. *That should do it.* Declan was due in half hour to pick her up for the volleyball game tonight.

If he comes, you mean. If he doesn't call to cancel again.

Baylyn shook her head at the thought. *He won't!*

Baylyn sighed as she looked at the clock. 45 minutes late. No phone call. No text message.

No Declan. Again.

She was adult enough to know that sometimes, Things Just Came Up. Perhaps this was one of those occasions. Declan had family in the area. Maybe there was a family emergency?

Even as the possibility rolled around in her brain, excusing him, she had the unwelcome and unbidden memory of Rob, her ex-boyfriend, doing the same thing which, ultimately, led to the exposure of The Big Secret. Too many excuses were given for not showing up for plans that were made ahead of time, like he did one too many times.

On the very last time that Rob stood her up, Baylyn had resolutely proceeded with going to the movie alone. The movie they were supposed to see together. The movie where she found Rob sitting two rows ahead of her, feeding some blond chick theater candy.

With his mouth.

The memory of it was enough to jar her into action. She and Declan were supposed to go play sand volleyball tonight. She was dressed and ready. Might as well just go, right?

I'll just go then. She stomped to the kitchen door, keys in hand, and decided at the last second to wait just ten more minutes.

Her mood was dark as she drove to the volleyball pits behind the high school. Alone. Great. Now the team they were supposed to sub for would be short one. Not to mention, she'd be fielding questions about Declan's absence.

Where the hell was he? She hoped for his sake he was hung up in a meeting. With a dead phone battery. And had already ordered flowers to go along with his apology. She fumed as she drove. It would be different if this were the *first* time.

However, it had happened several times now. The first few times were a fluke, she thought at first. The excuses were varied. Piece of equipment was vandalized. Something wrong with his car. There was a work emergency; something went wrong with a building permit. However, she had at least *heard* from him when he had cancelled before.

Not this time. But she had just spoken to him that morning! Their conversation, like all of them had been lately, was flirty. Breathy. Sexy. And she could have sworn she had reminded him about the volleyball game tonight.

Didn't she? She couldn't remember.

Cat jogged up to the car, ponytail swinging. "Where's Declan? Please tell me that he's on his way. If he's not coming, that Reynaud guy is going to take his place tonight. He showed up hoping there'd be an opening. That guy gives me the creeps. Tell me Declan's coming!"

"What? Why is he even here?" Bay jabbed in the general direction of Reynaud. "I can't stand him either. There's something really off about that guy." Baylyn peeked around Cat. Sure enough, there he was, looking in their direction. "He's asked me out twice already. Doesn't the guy take a hint? He's always hinting at things only 'we can do together' and staring at my chest. And Declan? Well, Declan is, uh...Declan had other plans tonight. Apparently."

Cat's sympathetic look both comforted and annoyed Baylyn.

"Cat, don't. It's not like that."

"What was it this time? Piece of equipment break? Another permit canceled? Late night meeting?"

Baylyn slowly shook her head.

"Did he call this time?" Baylyn shook her head again.

"Seriously? Not even a call? Text?"

"No, but..."

Cat looked at her sternly. "Do you remember this happening w...?"

"Don't even say it. Declan is not like that." Baylyn shook her head decisively. "He's not like Rob. At all."

They reached the volleyball pits. "Maybe so, but this is what, the fourth time it's happened? Put your foot down this time, Baylyn. I mean, you're worth a quick phone call."

"I know that." *I know that he should have called, or at least returned the calls I made to him tonight. I also know that I'm going to play hard tonight. Take my rage out on the court. While I ignore Reynaud. And what* amazing *timing that guy has. He seems to always show up when Declan can't make it. At the mall. At the park. Tonight, at the volleyball courts. Always watching me. Trying to talk to me. You'd think the amount of time I spend ignoring him, he'd get the hint.* She shuddered.

Baylyn's heart wasn't in the game tonight. She had some good plays, feeding spikes to other members of her team, but there were a few times she definitely had her head in the clouds. Her team won, but it seemed as if there were a couple of plays that should not have gone their way...a ball landing in bounds on the other team's side when it clearly looked as if it would sail several feet over the boundary line. A couple of spikes that teetered on the top of the volleyball net then fell on the other teams' side, when they should have fallen on her team's side.

Curious, and way too lucky, she thought, almost as if magic was being used. Bay did a self-check a couple of times to make sure it wasn't *her* magic causing the near misses and she could swear it wasn't. Perhaps it *was* just luck that caused her team to win each match.

To her disgust, Reynaud tried several times to talk to her. She politely ignored him. Ugh, she thought. *I've had it with that guy. Give it UP, dude!!*

On the way home, alone, Bay couldn't believe she still hadn't heard from Declan. She had far too much pride to call him, but that didn't keep her from scrolling back through any missed calls (none) and any text messages (just one, from Cat). Nothing.

She had a sick feeling in the pit of her stomach. Although she fought to keep them down, unsettling feelings and thoughts from the past were rising up, threatening to destroy her trust in Declan. The trust she had worked so hard to build. So what was going on?

Pulling into the grocery store to pick up bottled water, she gasped and realized that what was going on was that Declan was going to need a *really, really good excuse* for why she had just seen him coming out of the supermarket with a bottle of wine and a bouquet of flowers, talking on the phone.

Tears filled her eyes and before he could see her, she left. Bottled water could wait.

She was magnificent, thought Reynaud, watching Baylyn. *Magnificent.* She was sweating lightly during their volleyball match and Reynaud could barely concentrate on the game as he watched her as a hawk watches his prey. Strands of her dark hair were falling out of the messy ponytail she had gathered up. Her arms were young and strong, her legs; sleek and long. He wanted those long, long legs wrapped around him, and her waiting against his black silk sheets. Several times he flubbed a play but more than made up for it, halfheartedly using his magic to keep the ball in play or in bounds…but always to their benefit.

Baylyn might not have known that Declan was going to miss their date, but he sure did. After all, he was the one who sabotaged the work site tonight. It was really the perfect plan, making it look like a break-in, vandalizing equipment, smashing windows. He loved that the police would have to be involved, keeping Declan from attending the volleyball game. His favorite part was sending a fake text to Declan from Baylyn, telling him the volleyball game was rescheduled and good thing; because she really wasn't feeling well. *Going to bed. See you tomorrow?*

Genius. Pure genius.

He sensed the trust issues building in Bay; sometimes he was shocked that other people couldn't see what he saw. Of course, they didn't have the benefit of being able to scroll through someone's past like he did...pausing to take mental notes here and there about where Bay's issues resided. Like a movie.

He watched her closely during the volleyball match. She definitely was upset that Declan, sweet sweet Declan, wasn't coming tonight. Perhaps, given enough time and a couple more cancelled dates, those issues would come to a head and she'd give good ol' Declan the heave ho. *It's happening again*, she would think. *Rob, all over again.*

Time for Reynaud to ride to the rescue. To comfort Baylyn, of course. Comfort.

Comfort, and possess.

That Cat, though? He may need to get rid of that her. She was too protective. Too nosy for her own good.

Chapter 13

"Bay, what gives you the idea that I'm avoiding you? If I understand you correctly, that's what you think I'm doing. I've told you the truth every time." Declan looked honestly confused. "You couldn't be more wrong."

It was the day after the volleyball game. He had shown up with flowers and wine, as if *that* could make it better. She had clunked the wine into the liquor cabinet and grudgingly threw the flowers in a vase as he watched her, a quizzical look on his face, until she informed him that he must be avoiding her for some reason, like disinterest or *another girlfriend*, otherwise he would have called or something, anything, to let her know about this latest cancellation of plans.

Now he paced in her kitchen, making the airy room shrink to about one third its size.

Bay was momentarily startled by the emotion in his voice. *Yes, but I've heard all these excuses before, from Rob. He had appeared sincere, too. The whole time he telling her about working late or having a dead cell phone battery, he had been lying to her, stringing her along, and just biding time until he had funneled enough money away to rent a new place with his new girlfriend, Workinlate Cellbroke.*

She had let her guard down. She had avoided doing any sort of spying spells on Rob. Trust was a given, right? To that end, she decided she wouldn't work so much as a fidelity spell or a knot spell. If it was meant to be, it would be. That was pretty early on in their four year relationship. Later she found out about the girlfriend in the old fashioned way. Alone on another night due to "something that came up", she went to the movies with a friend. It was then that she saw Rob and some girl together.

Her heart gave a lurch as Declan stopped pacing and stood in front of her. He had never looked more like a young boy to her, with his tousled dark hair under a faded blue ball cap, his hands jammed into the pockets of his blue jeans, thumbs worrying the tops of the pockets.

She so badly wanted to believe him. She could feel herself melting.

Declan's eyes looked dark as he stood in front of her, hand on the wall behind her, the other in his pocket. He leaned forward. "Satisfy my curiosity. Why do you think I'm being dishonest? Wait. Let me guess. An old boyfriend. What did he do to you, Bay, that you have to paint me with the same brush? You should have thrown that brush away when you met me. You *know* me. What was his name?"

Bay could feel her magic perking up, coming to her defense. Behind him the teapot lifted off the stove and hung suspended, trembling.

She shushed it down. "Look at it from my point of view, Declan. I talk to you in the morning, tell you about the volleyball game. You're all excited, say you'll be there, whatever. And later, nothing. Not even a phone call. No text."

Declan rocked back on his heels, threw up his arms in frustration. "I told you what happened! I don't know what else to tell you! You texted me in the afternoon, saying the game was cancelled, and that was good, you were happy, because you were going to bed with a migraine. *Don't call,* you said. *Let you sleep,* you said."

Righteous, reckless anger boiled through Baylyn as her eyes flashed right back at him. Back up came the teapot. "Oh, right. Go through my cell phone, Declan. You'll find I didn't text you at all, just called you much later when you didn't show up for volleyball."

"For the third time, I didn't get any phone calls from you after that text. I was giving you some space because you said you had a massive headache. I was being considerate! You can check *my* phone!"

Baylyn fired back, emphasizing each word. "I don't think so." The teapot dropped back down on the stove with a loud thunk, causing Declan to flinch and turn around.

"I guess the house is settling," she told him blandly. "Here's the thing about trust, Declan. I think I've given you the benefit of the doubt. But it isn't just this time that's got me so frustrated. It's all these times." Now Bay was the one who was pacing. "We have a blast, we talk, whatever it is, then, nothing. Nothing until I get a cancellation call, if even that. I get it. I work, you work, and we're busy people. But the excuses are starting to pile up here. Now you blow me off and follow it with the excuse that I was the one to cancel? Give me a break. Trust? Once it's gone, it's gone. Once it's damaged, it takes a very long time to gain it back."

"Don't I know it." He muttered.

"I find it hard to believe any woman ever got the best of you."

He crossed the kitchen in long strides, and pulled her reluctant-but-unresisting self into his arms. "Do you think you're the only person who's ever had trust issues? Do you honestly think that even now, I'm not jealous of any man who has the balls to even give you a second glance?"

"Oh, please." She waved an arm.

She could feel, and then see the tension draining out of his body as he stood in front of her. "Bay, have you looked in the mirror lately?" He turned her whole body with his to look into the gilt framed mirror on the wall. "Look at you. You are so beautiful." He stood behind Baylyn, so near that she could feel his heat from head to toe. She studied Declan in the mirror.

"Your eyes, so blue. So clear. When you look at me, sometimes I could swear time stops and I just drown. Your perfect, long, curly hair…" he used both hands to fist great handfuls of curls, then tilted her head to the side, breathing warmly against her neck. Her knees were shaky as he forced her to watch him as he touched her.

"Your cute little ears. Like miniature seashells." He leaned forward a little more, angling his hard body to fit hers snugly, still watching her. He breathed in her ear before lightly kissing first one, then around the back of her head to kiss the other.

"Look at yourself," he whispered. See yourself as I see you. See why I'm almost afraid to let you out of my sight for even a moment. I'm jealous of every single person you talk to during the day. I don't know who hurt you, baby, but the man was a complete moron."

He tugged gently on her hair, pulling her head back against his solid chest. She was unable to do more than watch him.

"How do you think I could ever let someone like you get away? Or even take a chance of that by lying to you about where I am, when all I want to do is spend every single minute with you? I don't want to waste even one night away from you. It's excruciating. I had to stop myself from coming to your house last night anyway, just to lay with you and kiss away your headache.

"Bay, you're the last thing I want to see at night and the first thing I think about in the morning. I'm not going to risk that by "avoiding" you so I can go have a beer with the guys or hang out with some other girl. All I want is you." He buried his face in her hair and pulled her even closer to him.

"Rob" she whispered.

Declan stilled. "What did you say?"

"Rob. He was the one. Broke my heart. Made me gun-shy. I had thought we would get married. We were together for a while, and then lived together for a couple of years. He found someone else. The problem is, he didn't tell me anything about it. Didn't do the stand-up guy thing and just say, *hey, this isn't working out for me. I need to end it.*" Baylyn's words were muffled. "I didn't see it. He just kept giving me one excuse after another for why he just wasn't *there* anymore. I was a fool." Declan turned her around so that he could look into her eyes.

"He was the fool. Do you hear me? He was the fool. I'd like to find him and punch his lights out. Then, I'd shake his hand."

"What?"

"For letting you go. So that I could find you."

Parked down the road, pretending to be talking on his cell phone, Reynaud seethed. Although he couldn't hear the conversation Bay and Declan were having, he had thought it would go badly, due to all the broken plans of late. Surely her mistrust would be playing a big role in splitting the pair of them up. After all, her last long relationship ended because her boyfriend was cheating on her with another woman. She should know men are all the same. Declan was not to be trusted either. She couldn't be giving him another chance!

Declan should have been given the boot by now. Where was he? Why hadn't he come out of the house yet? Where was the yelling? The fighting? Don't tell me she forgave him...stupid girl.

Reynaud smoothed his eyebrow with his pinky, calming himself. He would break them up yet. And if that didn't work, there were quicker, albeit messier, ways to get Declan out of the picture. Bay would be his.

Chapter 14

In Baylyn's experience, a pet adoption day was not very well attended, no matter how many flyers were posted or ads taken out in the paper. Even if there were more prospective adoptees than normal, most of the people went home empty handed. This was Baylyn's third pet adoption day at Paws, the local animal shelter, and this was the busiest she had ever seen it.

Hopefully lots of dogs and cats would find their Forever Home today with their new owners.

It was a beautiful day. The sun was out and the library parking lot they were holding the adoption in had lots of tree cover, so where the sun did shine in it dappled everything with light.

It was in this light that Baylyn stood. She was holding a wiggly puppy that was 100% mutt and 100% adorable. Whatever he was, he was licking Baylyn's face joyfully while she was talking to prospective pet parents. Baylyn had to finally switch him to the other arm because—yuk—he had licked her open mouth twice. As much as she loved puppy breath, enough was enough.

"Thpu! Thpu! You and that tongue! You should audition for lead singer of the Rolling Stones, doggy. I'm going to call you Stony. Yes, I am." She leaned closer to the puppy and in a sing song voice repeated herself. "Yes, I am!"

Unbridled joy wrapped in a puppy body wriggled against her. And Baylyn thought for the hundredth time there was no sweeter smell than a puppy.

Her eyes cut a few tables over down the side of the parking lot, searching out and locating Declan, who was staring at her with an intensity that made her insides give a warm, loopy roll.

He was kneeling down with an aging yellow lab, smoothing her shiny coat over and over. A slow, sexy smile stole over his features as Baylyn's eyes made contact with his.

Oh, my. Baylyn thought faintly. *I do believe that smile was meant just for me.* She could practically feel her hair curling as she met his powerful gaze.

It seemed at that moment like every single thing in her world clicked into place. She felt a preternatural hush settle over her and her surroundings, blocking the sounds around her from reaching her ears; so when she heard and felt a powerful pause and thump of her heart, she knew her body was telling her something.

She was firmly rooted to the spot and couldn't have moved if she wanted to. *This is how it happens*, she thought, with a quiet certainty. Her very own heart's reaction seemed to have underlined her thoughts even as she had them.

You meet the right man and suddenly it's all easy. It all makes sense.

I love him. It seemed as if the words themselves were magic, and the scrolled letters of that phrase I love you were actually in front of her, written on gilded strips of paper, gliding, sliding, tilting this way and that, as if they were putting on a show just for her.

Baylyn thought back over all the years, thinking of the clichés she had heard.

Flowers smell sweeter.

Food tastes better.

The sun shone brighter.

The very air she breathed in seemed to be infused with some kind of…well…magic. She noticed him standing up and began walking over to her, and Baylyn could feel her cheeks pink as she sent him a smile of her own.

He absolutely takes my breath away.

Watching Baylyn, her sweet innocence, graceful demeanor and beautiful smile, Declan's mouth went dry. He felt as if he had stood staring for hours instead of minutes.

Man, she was something else.

Declan had never met anyone like her, ever. She was absolutely adorable and contrary to her own self—playing with puppies yet swearing like a sailor. Sitting across from him at dinner while under that sedate skirt was fire engine red lingerie and thigh highs.

She was the type of woman you don't let go, he mused, walking her way. Her smile lit a beacon in his heart that he knew would never be extinguished.

He would tell her soon, he thought. He would have to handle the timing very carefully—introduce her by bits and pieces and levels to the fact that he was, in fact, smitten; until she was completely comfortable with him. Everything seemed to him to be going so well; she was the most remarkable person he had ever met and yet he could tell he needed to tread lightly when talking with her about a deeper relationship as she looked like a scared little kitten when their future came up. His feelings for her were now sure. Powerful. If she didn't feel the same way about him yet, he would wait however long it took.

He wanted to see her with their puppy, in front of their home, where they were about to go in and make dinner with a little salt, a little pepper, and a little kiss. Or a big one. Or many, many kisses and just forget the damn dinner. He could feel his eyebrow rising of its own accord in time with his lascivious thoughts.

"Nick! Nicky! Baby, where are you?" The same woman's shriek interrupted his pleasant train of thought. She had been calling for a minute or so, her voice beginning to sound more panicky.

Suddenly the wild-eyed woman was in front of him, looking around frantically. "Have you seen my son? He's just two and a half. He got out of the stroller when I wasn't looking, I have to find him, there's a road…" She trailed off as her face went white. "Oh, no, the road!" She whirled on her heel, single minded in her determination to find her boy.

Declan looked up to where the woman was headed—and his heart dropped. There was the little tyke, following hot on the heels of a balloon that had escaped, paying little attention to the fact that just feet away was a busy street and he was headed directly for it.

The mother had seen her son at the same time, but there was no way she was going to close the distance in time—and they were more than 100 yards away from the impending disaster.

Declan didn't think, he just reacted. He broke into a full out run and when it became obvious he would not get there in time, he threw all he had into his body to try to stop the boy from certain death.

Everything froze. Declan felt his legs straining and arms pumping in full stride, his lungs raggedly bringing in air to his lungs. Noises stopped and the quiet was deafening. It was surreal. Traffic seemed halted whereas they were booking along moments before, and people were rooted in place, caught in the act of whatever they had been doing, as if frozen where they stood. Declan rushed to the boy, pulled his unresisting body backward, and the two of them tumbled on the grass. He spared a glance up at the crowd attending the pet adoption. They too were locked into place. *What was going on here?*

Even his lovely Baylyn was motionless, hands over her face.

Moments later, it seemed time caught up. Sounds flooded his ears as the traffic screamed by. The little balloon chaser, Nick, began crying over finding himself right next to a stranger on the grass and away from his mother, who was running to him at top speed. The crowd at the adoption fair all faced the street, their hands blocking the sun as they peered at mom and son's reunion.

She burst into tears as she reached down and hauled the little boy into a tight embrace, kissing him all over even as she tearfully admonished him for running away. "You scared mommy. You can't leave your stroller without holding mommy's hand, remember?"

She paused in her scolding long enough to look at Declan. "I never saw anyone move so fast in my entire life." Through tears and loud kissing noises from the kisses on her son's head, she thanked Declan profusely. "I don't understand how you did it!"

Neither do I, thought Declan. He stood, slightly leaned over, his hands bracing on his thighs. His lungs burned, his thighs burned. He looked back at the parking lot, and then turned to the road. There was just no possible way he had made it to the road on time. He had heard of bursts of energy, but this was more. Why had everything looked like it was frozen? Why had traffic actually stopped, and people too, midstream in talking and conversation? It was the biggest question of the day, the fact that everyone in the world seemed to be frozen except him.

Baylyn was in shock.

Her pulse was out of control from the spell she cast on the onlookers.

Baylyn had watched Declan walk toward her with his long limbed stride. So handsome. So tall. So focused on her. So flipping awesome. Hers.

She saw when his attention was drawn to the little boy running after the balloon. Saw him running. Saw that he would never make it…the little one had a significant head start.

She watched him running—running—and threw up her hands in horror, her mind forming a spell so quick she wasn't consciously aware she had done it. She could see through her splayed fingers Declan's full out spring, watched as time stood still. He ate up the distance between him and the boy, grabbing him and falling backward onto the grass. The boy had been mere inches from the straight truck bearing down on him. Declan had saved him from certain death.

Thank God. The words still burned on her tongue and the spell rattled around in her brain.

But Declan was going to know something was off. How would she handle that conversation? Maybe she'd be all casual about it. "By the way, I can help you understand what happened. I just threw out a *time stoppage* spell, that's all. Didn't I mention I was a witch?" Oh, sure. She had tried so hard to be more normal around Declan. Sure, she used her magic for little things, but this? She couldn't hide this had happened. What could she possibly…

The bowling alley.

She had cast a spell at the bowling alley, hadn't she, to help people forget they saw a bowling ball hovering in the air? She knew people had seen that happen, and had whispered a little *forgetfulness* spell. No one was the wiser.

He was walking back up the slope now, behind the red-eyed mother and her squalling runaway. What could she say to him? His eyes looked as though he was searching for her. What would she say? She felt as though she was betraying him. It suddenly boiled up in her chest.

It was now or never. Be truthful or…maybe she just needed a little more time. She shut her eyes and whispered the spell that would prevent onlookers from questioning anything had happened; for all they knew, Declan had all the time in the world to get to the little boy.

Even as she did, however, she felt so guilty. Lies. Deceit. Betrayal. Isn't that what Rob had done to her? Lied to her, hid things? Betrayed her when she was sure he was telling the truth about who he was? Her hands slowly dropped to her sides. She could feel her throat closing up, a hard hot lump forming. She closed her eyes, hurting. He would not see her cry. Then he would want to comfort and hold her and she could not bear it.

She would make a deal with herself that he would never find out about her powers. She could change who she was for the man she loved. Small price. She refused to lie to the one she loved.

Baylyn watched as Declan shook the little boys' hand solemnly, warning against future field trips without mom. He accepted a grateful hug from the mom and headed Baylyn's way.

"Are you ok?" Baylyn breathed. "What was that all about?" Even as she spoke the words they felt sour in her mouth.

"I have no earthly idea. I know this sounds really insane…" Declan ran fingers through his hair, appearing both frightened and frustrated. "…but there's no way in hell I could have made it to that kid in time. It was almost like time stopped. But that's ridiculous. It must have been in my head, just felt that way. There's just no way…time didn't actually stop, I know. Couldn't have."

"You're a hero, Declan. You saved that little boy. It doesn't really matter how, it just matters that you did it."

Declan looked back at her. "You know, when we fell back on the grass, I looked up toward the crowd and no one was moving. Nothing was moving. Everything just seemed frozen. Even you, Baylyn." He rubbed a tired hand over his face. "I haven't gotten much sleep. I have been working too much and maybe I just imagined something." He reached for Baylyn, pulled her into his warm arms, and rested his chin on her head. "I'm sure that's all it was. Geez, everything happened so fast, I almost don't remember it. It's bizarre!"

Yeah, weird.

"Want to get out of here? Go get some dinner?" Declan looked at her expectantly.

With your cowardly girlfriend? "That depends. Which dog or cat is going home with you?"

"You drive a hard bargain. Looks like Dori's getting a brother or sister. And you, woman…you're getting pizza at the house."

As they drove away, Declan's new senior yellow lab stuck her head out the truck window and into the wind, slowly wagging her tail.

The shovel made a decisive sound as over and over, it cut through the chilly earth under the big tree in Baylyn's back yard. This was a little more work than she had planned on.

"Why are you digging that hole?" The little blonde imp was very careful to stay in her back yard, like her momma had probably asked her to. She leaned as far as she could over the fence in order to watch Baylyn.

"That's a pretty big hole."

It was early October, Baylyn's favorite time of year. Darkness was coming earlier and earlier at night, the leaves were turning beautiful colors, and the evening and early morning air had a delicious chill to it.

It had rained several times during the week, making the ground softer than normal but not as soft as she hoped it would be. Baylyn looked over at her next door neighbor's precocious little girl.

"It's going to rain again today, Amanda." she said, changing the subject.

Amanda was not letting it go. "What's going to go in there? Are you planting a tree? Are you planting a bush? I like flowers. Are you planting those? Are you going to bury pirate treasure?" Baylyn wasn't surprised at the question, as Amanda was wearing an eye patch to match her striped pirate vest. She couldn't wait for Halloween.

"Why, do you have some treasure for me to bury?" Baylyn teased. The little girl shook her head, her visible eye shining at the thought.

She rested a booted foot on the shovel head. "Well, Amanda, if you're putting something big into the ground, you need to dig the hole big enough, right?"

"I guess so." Amanda spun around in a circle on one heel, humming a song to herself.

Taking a break from her digging, Baylyn watched the little girl, feeling jealous of her youth and enthusiasm. Amanda knew who she was. She knew without question that her mother and father loved her, she had a new swing set, a dog named Champ, and that she was going to be a pirate for Halloween. She was in first grade this year. Those were the things that made up Amanda.

Baylyn had no idea what made up *Baylyn*, though. She was a witch, sure, but that was only one tiny aspect of her personality. Baylyn wasn't sure she wanted the dubious honor of even being a witch. What made up the rest? Who *exactly* was Baylyn Travers? At times she felt bereft of any purpose or direction. She had no dog or swing set, although she was relatively certain that if she asked Amanda if she could swing with her, the answer would be a resounding yes.

Her friend and co-worker Cat knew exactly who she was and what she wanted. It had come at some cost, Baylyn knew. Cat knew without a shadow of a doubt that she would get married when the right guy came along and raise 2.5 kids with that man. She knew what kind of house she wanted to live in and already drove the car she wanted, a Dodge Charger.

Cat wore gray or black pants almost every day because everything matches with black or gray, and her favorite shoes she wore were a pair of black penny loafers. She was also the only person Baylyn knew who actually *liked* their hair and never seemed to have a bad hair day. In short, Cat was comfortable with herself day in and day out. She knew who she was.

Baylyn was all over the board, with her outfits and most other things. Some days begged for a plaid skirt with tights and long dark hair wound into a severe bun. Comfortable and straitlaced. Other days called for black high heels and a blouse with a pleasantly sassy neckline, wavy hair free of pins and barrettes. Comfortable and free.

Baylyn hoped to be married one day too. She knew she could do this for Declan. It had only been a short time, but deep inside she felt as if her soul had recognized its match in Declan. She hoped he felt the same way. He seemed to love being around her, and often he had told her how much he liked how real she was with him. Would that change if she gave up the small part of her that was magic? Would she be less real to him, or more so?

How about when she turned 30? When she turned 30, her magic wasn't going to be a small part of her anymore. Controlling her power was already hard at times, especially around Declan. When the full measure of her magic came in, it would be difficult, if not impossible to rein in.

She sighed and looked at Amanda, with her blonde hair scraped into those tiny blonde pigtails, her heart warmed. She vaguely remembered that age. Even then she was getting in trouble for using her magic.

Something was different about today. Baylyn blinked a few times and moments later, remembered. It dawned on her with a giggle that it was her birthday. *I'm 7 today*, she thought, as she lay in her bed under the covers.

She happily wiggled her toes.

Today, her mother would bake a yummy chocolate cake with strawberry icing, because on your birthday, you got whatever kind you wanted, and that was her favorite.

A shiver of excitement went through her. Since it was her birthday, she'd get to choose her birthday meal, which of course was McDonalds. She already had $5 in birthday money. Her mother said that she could spend it on anything she wanted. Baylyn thought she'd really like to get a Rolo McFlurry and some nail polish like her babysitter wore.

Her mother had called the party guests, four girls from her class, to invite them for cake and ice cream and games later.

She'd help mommy clean the house like a big girl, in preparation for her party. She'd help blow up balloons and last but not least, she would get to make the birthday wish she'd been waiting for all year long, waiting for this special day.

Her day passed in a flurry of activity, and before she knew it, party guests were arriving. Her friends were all sweaty and red faced with the exertion of running around playing before her mother yelled, "Here it is!"

She came around the corner of the snack bar holding Baylyn's special cake, lit with 7 candles.

Someone turned off the kitchen lights, enhancing and heightening Baylyn's excitement. Everyone gathered around her.

As they sang Happy Birthday to her, she closed her eyes in joy and as the last line was sung, Baylyn crossed all her fingers and wished as hard as she could. She nodded with satisfaction and blew out the candles.

Nothing happened. Baylyn shot glances around the kitchen and the living room while her mother was serving cake. No evidence of her wish was seen. Her friend Amy asked her what she had wished for. Baylyn just smiled and shook her head. She knew that if you told someone what your wish was, you would have no chance of it coming true.

She carefully opened presents, admiring little toys, stuffed animals and new crayons.

Later, as the last of the party guests gathered their coats and said goodbye, Baylyn rushed to her room, unable to wait even one more second to check again on her wish. Much to her disappointment, not a thing had changed. Her Barbies were still lined up exactly like they were, accessories stored neatly in the special Barbie wardrobe. Still immobile. Still plastic.

Still not alive, even though that was her special birthday wish.

I guess it's just not going to happen.

Wish a sigh, she turned off the lights and left the room to watch TV.

Later, she was tucked into bed with hair damp from her bath, wearing her brand new Barbie pajamas, in her Barbie sheets.

Her mother leaned over and kissed her forehead.

"Did you have a good day? Get everything you wanted?"

Baylyn sighed sleepily. "Almost everything."

Her mother chuckled, adjusted the covers with a final pat. "Night, now."

Baylyn eyed her Barbies longingly until she her eyes could not stay open one more minute. Nothing happened.

A few hours later, however, she awoke to hear a rustling sound. Then another. Then the sound she was certain she'd never hear—her Barbies were happily talking to each other, whispering and laughing.

Baylyn was so excited she jumped from her bed and flipped the lights on.

It was true. Baylyn's entire collection of over 50 Barbies was doing flips, turning cartwheels and dancing. There were several looking excitedly over the new Barbie clothes Baylyn received for her birthday. Several were combing their long, long Barbie hair.

"Oh my goodness! Oh my goodness! My friends!" Baylyn whispered, jumping up and down, turning this way and that way in astonishment.

Baylyn and her Barbies played throughout the night. Several Barbies combed her hair and styled it this way and that with their little hands. They laughed as they instructed Baylyn to try on this outfit or that, and then had an enormous tea party.

Every single Barbie accessory was on the floor in disarray, as hours later, an exhausted Baylyn yawned hugely.

Tenderly, the gaggle of Barbies tucked her in, their tiny voices murmuring lovingly as they smoothed her hair and lined up one by one to give her kisses on the cheek.

"I love you, Barbies." Baylyn whispered sleepily. "This was by far the most fun ever. You all are so sweet and so fun to play with. I knew you would be."

Baylyn fell asleep with a smile on her face.

The next morning, Baylyn's mother woke her up with tone in her voice that she hadn't heard many times before…only when her mother was angry. What could she have to be angry about? Baylyn shuffled out to the kitchen, rubbing her eyes.

"Hi, mommy."

Her mother turned to her, disappointment visible in her eyes.

"Baylyn. Did you use magic last night? All I could smell was magic when I got up."

Baylyn's eyes were shining. "Mommy, you should have seen them! My Barbies were so sweet and nice and fun."

Elise sat down at the table with Baylyn, grabbing her hands in her own larger ones. "Your powers are growing faster than I had thought they would, baby. Not everyone is comfortable with our magic, sweetie. It would be a good idea if you didn't do that anymore."

"Like, no magic ever?"

Her mother looked away. "I'm not forbidding it, Baylyn. I'm just telling you, as a big girl now, that you absolutely must be careful who you show your powers to from now on. Family, that's fine. Other witches we know, that's fine. No showing off, though. The important thing to remember is to not do spells around people who aren't gifted like we are, ok?"

Baylyn was still confused. "It was a birthday wish, mommy. I wished on the candles that my Barbies would come alive. And they did. I didn't do magic."

"Actually, that IS your magic, honey. Your powers are young and still coming in, and that's why it didn't happen immediately, but later, after everyone went to bed. I could smell it in the air. It's like the smell of a fresh orange blossom."

She rested her chin on her hands on the top of the shovel. She knew she was a witch, but sometimes it didn't feel like it was true. Baylyn felt sometimes that she was only playing at being a witch. She didn't feel much like a witch. How was a witch supposed to feel? It seemed that there was always something she was missing about the whole magic community. She was familiar with the traditions. She knew the spells, even if she didn't cast them often for herself or for others. She didn't wear the traditional witch garb that some witches still wore on high holidays.

Sure, she could do some parlor tricks. If she *thought* the coffee mug into her hand, the coffee mug *appeared* in her hand, even if she was in the other room. She could even do it now without spilling a drop, after lots of practice. She still made her bed by hand, but if she wanted to, she could wave one lazy hand and the bed would make itself. The biggest spell she'd done lately was the time stoppage spell, which had surprised even her with its success. Obviously her powers were strengthening.

Amanda interrupted her daydreaming. "I'm a pirate. Do you like my costume?"

Baylyn walked over and leaned on the fence. "I *love* your costume, Amanda. Are you Jack Sparrow?"

"No, I'm Amanda, silly. What are *you* going to be for Halloween?" she asked Baylyn.

Baylyn pretended to think about it long and hard, rubbing her chin.

"I'll be a witch."

The little girl jumped and clapped her hands. "I told my mom that's what you were going to be."

"You did?" she tousled the little girl's hair gently.

"I knew you'd be a witch. A good witch, though, right?"

"It's the only kind I know how to be." Baylyn said thoughtfully. What if. What if Declan could continue to accept her for who she was? He didn't need to know about her powers. She could keep them from him. All witches had the choice to be good or evil; there hadn't been an evil witch in Bay's family for over 20 generations. It wasn't going to start now. She just needed to get her act together before she turned 30 and her magic grew exponentially. Her powers would be stronger; her abilities stronger. If she could get her emotions under control, Declan would never know.

She wasn't like Rob. This wasn't a choice, something she was doing to spite Declan.

This was who she was. And he liked who she was. She liked who she was. Her posture straightened and she took in a cleansing breath. It was true, she did like who she was. Magic and all.

"You didn't tell me what the hole is for, Miss Baylyn." asked the tiny pirate.

Baylyn looked over to the small trunk under the base of the tree, nearly hidden from sight. It contained her spell book, certain small charms she could use to work spells, a special pendant, a mortar and pestle, and various special engraved bowls. Tonight, she had all intentions to bury it. She was not sure she wanted to acknowledge her destiny. She thought she wasn't ready.

Maybe, though, it *was* time to embrace all that it meant. Maybe she was ready. Only by truly embracing who she was would she be truly herself with Declan.

I need to trust him. How unfair that I think Declan's withholding secrets from me, when I'm holding something this big back from him. I need to trust myself. I need to trust in us.

I am a witch.

She was surprised at the sudden pride. Her eyes teared a little with the whispered pronouncement.

"Well, you see…" Baylyn walked back over to her shovel, picked it up, and began shoveling dirt back into the hole.

"I thought I needed it, but I don't."

Chapter 15

"Declan! Yoo-hoo, Declan!"

Stepping quickly down the front steps of the library, fresh on the heels of seeing his lady love, Declan came to a screeching halt. That voice.

"Declan! Over here!"

His heart sank. It couldn't be.

It was.

He resumed his descent faster now, hoping maybe he could skirt the impending conversation he did not want to have with a woman he did not want to see.

Boy, she was fast. The little blonde finished parking her car, rolled the window up she was yelling out of and clickity clacked her way over to him as quickly as her small, annoying feet could carry her.

Breathless, she stood in front of him. "Hi! I thought maybe you couldn't hear me and that's why you kept going!"

Close.

"And of all the places to run into you—the library! In all the time we dated I don't remember you ever even picking up a little old book."

Worst six months of my life. And you never saw me reading because you had your nose in front of a mirror all the time, primping...checking...patting...

"I read all the time." Declan said mildly. He stood there awkwardly for a few moments as Crystal processed the information, a vacuous expression on her face. He could see the instant the information hit her brain. She reached forward and gave his arm a surprisingly uncomfortable punch.

A little anger there, then.

"Oh, you teaser!" She laughed. "I ran into your mom the other day." Blink. Blink. "She always liked me." Crystal put extra emphasis on the word she. "She mentioned the party or gala or ball or whatever coming up—told me she had a spot at her table if I'd like to go."

How could I have wasted even one week with Crystal? Had it been boredom, or was it just apathy?

"Are you going?" Belatedly, Declan realized she was speaking to him.

"To the gala? I'm not sure but it's a possibility." Declan distractedly looked past her to his car and fingered his keys.

"Awesome! Awesome! I'll see you there, then? Your mother will probably have us sitting together." She grabbed a curl of her hair and worried it between her fingers. "It should be just like old times." She gave Declan a brilliant smile and shrugged her shoulders in. She reached out and touched his arm. It was a smooth, practiced move he had seen dozens of times from her before.

"I'll be sitting with Baylyn. She's organizing it."

"Baylyn?" Crystal tilted her head, looking confused. Her hand stilled.

Warning bells went off in his head but before he could say anything, her eyes narrowed. "Who is this Baylyn?" Crystal's words came out clipped.

"Baylyn is the librarian here. Baylyn Travers. Do you know her?"

The transformation on her face was instantaneous and almost comical. Crystal laughed. "Oh, the librarian. I thought maybe you were telling me that it was a girlfriend or something. Not a dowdy old librarian! What is she, a friend of your mothers or something?" She leaned in conspiratorially. "Old hen needs a new rooster to make her feel better for the night?"

"She's not old, she's not dowdy; she's stunning, actually. And she's my girlfriend."

The smile slid off Crystal's face in an instant.

"You have been dating someone else? You have a *girlfriend?*" She spat the last word, her volume increasing with each sentence. "Barely waited for the door to hit me in the butt before going off and shacking up with the...the...librarian?" She dragged the word librarian out as if it were a dirty word.

She has teeth like Chiclets. Did she always have teeth like Chiclets?

Declan sighed inwardly. He supposed this had to come up sometime...it was not a large city, after all. They were bound to run into each other. Too bad it was today, though. He was capping off the wonderful lunch date he had just enjoyed with Baylyn by trying to calm a hysterical ex. Lovely.

He took a few deep breaths. "*Crystal.* First off, we haven't dated in over six months, so as far as letting the door hit you in the butt, it would have to be a very, very slow closing door. Secondly, Bay and I are not "shacking up", as you so elegantly put it. We are dating, and it is none of your business." He punctuated each word with a sharp pause. Somehow he needed to get the message through to her.

At the word "business" he was realized he was talking to her back, because she had turned and flounced off the steps of the library, heels tapping. He almost laughed out loud as he saw her hand up, giving him the universal signal of 'I'm not listening anymore'. He could hear her mutter, but could only make out the snarled word *librarian.*

Well, that went well. Declan stared after her for a moment, feeling a little guilty. Not because Crystal was upset but for the fact that he realized he had dated her simply out of convenience.

Without question, Crystal was a looker. She was a quintessential blonde beauty—petite, tan, very easy on the eyes. They had met at his brother's baseball game. She was cute, he was lonely. As the weeks went on, they both tended to be at the same events and they fell into dating almost by accident. It became habit more than anything else.

He did neither of them any favors, he could see that now. Looking back, he was embarrassed that he hadn't just ended it far sooner, but at the time, he was busy with work and hadn't the time or energy for the drama he was certain Crystal would bring.

In the end, it came to a natural conclusion for him. Declan had lost his phone at a job site somewhere. When he bought a new one and began adding the contacts, he realized couldn't even remember Crystal's number. She had always called him. Arranged the dates. She did all the work, and he just went along with it.

If their relationship meant anything, wouldn't it have been second nature to put her number in first? Before his favorite pizza delivery place? It occurred to him just how little she meant to him and in the end, he just left her number out. Oddly, her calls seemed to have first slowed, and then stopped right around that time.

Shortly after that, he found out something Crystal had taken great pains to hide…and that was the fact she was two timing him with one of the guys from his brother's baseball team. Strange how things work out.

Reynaud was sitting inside the library "doing research" which was his term for keeping tabs on Baylyn. He had arrived earlier only to find that Baylyn had left with Declan to go to lunch, so he grabbed a couple of books (never looking at the titles) and waited at a table conveniently close to her office. And so he waited, until she returned with Declan. His stomach roiled as he watched her place a soft kiss on Declan's lips before he left the library.

Neither one noticed him.

A lunch date. How quaint. Reynaud was seething. How many times had he successfully fouled things up in Declan's life so that Declan had to either be late or leave before the end of a date? A couple of times, Reynaud had sabotaged the job site enough that Declan had to cancel with Bay altogether.

And yet she still stays with him. What was it going to take for his Bay to realize Declan was not the man for her? He idly flipped the pages of the book he had blindly grabbed off the shelf.

Frustrated, he looked down at the page. One word stuck out at him, "jealousy." He flipped the book to see the cover. It was a parenting book entitled *I'm a Big Brother Now*.

Jealousy. Surely not what he was experiencing—not him. What did he need to feel jealous of? Why, he was merely biding his time until that caveman Declan showed his true colors and Bay dumped him. It wouldn't be long.

Jealousy. A scene outside caught his interest with the woman's raised voice. He waved his hand so that he could overhear the conversation once he realized it was Declan himself with a lovely lady. His power to overhear at a distance came in handy from time to time and it certainly did in this case.

A sinister grin spread over his features as he took note of Declan looking more and more uncomfortable with the beautiful blonde.

"Well what do we have here?" Reynaud whispered to himself. *She seemed a little slow on the uptake, that one...unable to take a hint, apparently. Slow was good. Very, very good, in this situation.*

Jealousy. He played with the cover of the book. Big brothers weren't the only ones who could get jealous, were they?

No, sometimes jealousy was a perky stupid blonde who used to date your boyfriend. *And probably would very much like to again*, he thought, as he watched her storm away.

An idea formed.

Leaving the unread books on the table, he took one long, possessive glance back at Baylyn, animatedly talking to Cat. Probably about *that man.*

Don't worry, Baylyn, Reynaud thought. *You won't get hurt by that one. I'll make sure of it. I just have to make you see how untrustworthy he is. How unhappy he will make you, but how happy I will make you.*

He hurried out of the library after the blonde woman. She was just the thing he needed...perfect for driving a wedge between Baylyn and Declan.

Jealousy.

Crystal talked to herself as she stood at the counter at the dry cleaners. "He's not done with me yet." she muttered to herself. "Baylyn. What a stupid name for a stupid librarian. She's probably old and fat." Her favorite little black dress, the one that did wonderful things for her figure, was ready to be picked up. "I'll wear this to the damn gala. When he sees this dress, he'll remember everything about me he liked and she'll be just a memory."

"So are you okay? I saw you having an argument a few minutes ago. You seem a little distracted."

Crystal eyed the nondescript man standing next to her at the counter with disdain. Really? Who the hell was this? She decided to ignore him. Perhaps he would fly away like the little bug he was. Ignoring a man usually let him know exactly where he stood. And Crystal was an expert at ignoring.

She stared straight ahead although held herself a little more stiffly than she normally would as she felt his eyes looking her over.

The man tried again. "I know Declan, I know his type. Are the two of you an item?"

None of your goddamn business. Crystal was used to male attention and lots of it, but something about this man was unnerving. She was irritated and late and didn't have time for a lame pick up line.

"I'm sorry. Have we met?" Although he stood a good six inches above her, she did her best to look down her nose at him. To the clerk, she said, "Three blouses, two shirts. One black dress. Last name Fife. And you better hope they're done right this time."

"You don't know me, but I have the feeling we're going to be very good friends." Reynaud slid his forearm on the counter and centered his attention on Crystal.

Wrong, buster. She gave him an imperious look. To tell the truth, she was a little taken aback at the man's boldness.

He just stood there, cell phone in one hand, keys in another, smiling cockily at her.

What the hell? She sniffed haughtily and turned her head.

"That's not going to work on me, sweetheart. I think you and I need to go have a drink. We have more in common than you think."

Just as the clerk took her credit card and handed her the items, Crystal felt an odd feeling come over it. It was a peculiar sensation, like the feeling she got when whiskey hit her stomach, except this feeling spread over her scalp and down into her chest. *I should go have a drink with this guy. He looks like he could be fun, I guess. He seems really nice, actually.*

She gave her head a little shake. "What makes you think we have anything in common?" She meant for the question to come out more sharply than it did.

"Baylyn Travers."

Crystal was struck speechless. Why would this man know anything about Baylyn Travers? She had the persistent feeling that something wasn't right. Did he say he knew Declan? The tingling sensation ran over her scalp again as she stood there with her dry cleaning. She had to know what they had in common.

"What about her? From what I understand she's just a librarian. No biggie."

"You want Declan to stop seeing her. I want Declan to stop seeing her."

Crystal raised her eyebrows and tapped her perfectly manicured nails on the hangers. "You have my attention."

Just the thought of another woman touching Declan made her frustrated and angry. She had stopped at his house hoping to catch up with him. Getting an invite from his mother was perfect. Now they'd be able to have some drinks, do some dancing and get back together. She hadn't even imagined Declan would be dating anyone, let alone The Librarian. The thought of eliminating what she considered to be her only competition—now, that might be worth enduring this one's company for a bit. Hear him out. What harm could it do? *And if it meant getting rid of this Baylyn girl…make her jealous…*

"I doubt I have much to worry about."

Reynaud lowered his voice. "Oh, but you do. She's not just a librarian. She's truly the most beautiful woman I have ever laid eyes on. And I've seen them together. You do have much to worry about, my dear. Oh, but you do." Her scalp tingled again. She blinked slowly.

"Fine. One drink."

"Beautiful and smart. Two qualities I love."

Reynaud smiled to himself. *That certainly was easy. It helps when there's very little between the ears. Confident in her beauty, sure she's better than others. This one was a peach.*

She would prove to be a big help to him in the time to come…he had all *sorts* of tasks Crystal could help him with. He would make sure she felt it was all to win back her man, of course.

He giggled. *She would think that every single one of them were her own idea. It was going to be so much fun having a little puppet.*

Chapter 16

Bay was supposed to be making lists tonight. A list of what she needed at the grocery store (yogurt, lettuce, cat food, tea bags) and another list of books she wanted to order for the library.

She hemmed and hawed, staring at the computer, well-intentioned but too scatterbrained to actually commit anything to paper.

She clicked on a major library ordering website, and the man on the cover of one of the books caught her eye; the jawline was Declan's. The song that came on the radio immediately after that was a song she heard on the radio getting ready for a date with Declan.

I give up! Baylyn threw up her hands in exasperation. She was trying to concentrate, really she was. The minute she sat down at her kitchen table, the only thing she could think about was Declan. Lately, everything always came back to Declan.

They had been dating for several months now. Despite his stress from work lately and some missed dates, she felt things were going very, very well. It was so easy to be with him. What surprised her most was not that he was easy to get along with. She had been friends with several men, and it was enjoyable. But this? This was different. She could joke with him as a best friend, and yet, the physical attraction was driving her crazy.

Did he think of her the same way? She thought he did. She'd catch him looking at her, thoughtfully, before he gave her an easy smile. What was he thinking? Dammit, he was so fun to be with, so easy to get along with, so sexy he took her breath away—the kisses they had shared had started turning into more and more each time.

She was starting to think that things with Declan were different. She was starting to think she could trust him. What could this mean for them?

Declan. She rolled her mouth around the syllables, giving in to the daydream. She wasn't getting anything done anyway.

Declan. She said it out loud, liking the way it echoed in the empty room. She doodled on the open notebook sitting on the table. The grandfather clock marked the hour: one, two, three o'clock, all the way up to nine o'clock. *Dec-lan. Dec-lan,* she thought, along with the chiming of the clock.

Declan, she sing-songed, smiling like a fool.

It was new, this feeling. She leaned over the notebook, swirling her pen around and around, looping, creating leaves and vines, leaves and vines, hearts and leaves and vines. Her long hair brushed the paper on either side, making slight scratching noises; dark hair against the white paper, forming a little curtain around her as she allowed herself to daydream a little bit more.

His lips. Oh, his lips—strong and firm on hers—exactly right. Soft, dark stubble on his cheeks, chin, and upper lip—ohmygodhowsexy. Desire curled up in her belly at the thought. Those strong hands, how he held her to him as if the two of them were one, and that one naughty wicked hand of his always sneaking around to give her a firm squeeze, pulling her forward to him. Promising.

The way he smelled—all unique to only him—the faint smell of his clean, curly hair, his cologne, and the air exhaled from his lungs just as he was about to claim her mouth. That. That was the absolute best part of his kisses. She smiled dreamily, looking off into the distance, leaves and vines and hearts forgotten.

The jangling of the house phone was like a pitcher of cold water over her head. She jumped up, barking her knee hard on the kitchen table in the hurry to answer it.

"Hello?" she said crossly. She didn't like having her thoughts interrupted, especially these types of thoughts and it caused her to crack her knee besides. She grimaced and swore.

"Want me to kiss it for you?"

"*What?* Who is this?" The old rotary phone in the kitchen didn't have anything as newfangled as caller id.

"I said do you want me to kiss that knee for you?" The low, sexy male voice held a note of humor. Recognition dawned on her. Declan. "You're here?" she squeaked.

"Over here. Kitchen door."

She whipped her head around. Holy crap, speak of the devil, he really was here. She could see him waving at her through the curtain on the door.

"Yes. Do you think maybe we could hang up the phone and continue this conversation in person?" He held up a pizza box so she could see it. He tilted his head and wriggled his eyebrows at her.

"Ooooh! Oh, of course!" She smiled at him a few beats more, feeling a little disconnected. After all, mere minutes ago they had been kissing on her kitchen floor. In her head.

Feeling foolish and more than a little shy for some reason, she opened the door all the way, letting him in. A breeze from outside gently tousled her hair, bringing with it the mouthwatering smell of pepperoni. Her stomach grumbled. His nearness made her knees weak and her head spin.

She wobbled over to the cabinet and got out paper plates, napkins, a bottle of red wine and two glasses. Arms full, she turned around and her heart jumped crazily into her throat. She drank him in, greedy for the sight of him, and suddenly she was not hungry for anything but the man standing in front of her.

Declan had placed the pizza box on the table and was standing there, watching her. He was leaning with one hand on the back of the kitchen chair she had just vacated, other hand casually resting on his hip. Long legs were crossed at the ankle, and his mouth was quirked in a strange little half smile.

He was gorgeous. Baylyn couldn't quite catch her breath. She nervously tucked her hair behind her ear and looked down…oh, for crying out loud, she was in her pajama shorts and a t-shirt? Well, of course, because she had only gotten out of the shower half hour ago. And of course, no makeup. She looked up, a rueful grin on her face.

The conversational tone he used belied his words. "I couldn't stay away. I tried. I turned off the radio so I wouldn't be disturbed by songs that made me think of you. I forced myself to work on dry, boring contracts. I did sit ups. I did pushups. But Baylyn…" He let go of the chair. "I couldn't get you out of my head."

He advanced toward her. "I kept hearing your voice. Your voice, saying my name." He took another step, catlike, stalking her. "Over, and over, and over. Softly. Declan. Declan."

Her mouth went completely dry and the thudding in her chest sped up to complement the roaring in her ears.

"As a matter of fact, I could feel you, calling to me. Beckoning me. Drawing me here. Well, I listened, Baylyn. I'm here. I had to come. What, exactly, do you want with me?"

She blinked at him, dazed, but found her voice. Her voice was horse but brave as she told him, "Um, I could think of a few things, I think."

He stood in front of her now, wrapping one of his big hands in her long hair while the other he laid alongside her jaw, brushing the pad of his thumb over her bottom lip. His eyes were hypnotic, holding her hostage with nothing but his hungry gaze and spellbinding words.

"I could think of more than a few things to do, Baylyn. He leaned close to gently kiss her ear, his breath warm on her cheek. Let's start with this, shall we?" She swallowed hard, finding it hard to breathe.

"Yes."

"Yes, *what*, Baylyn?" Declan feathered soft kisses down the side of her jaw. His mouth hovered over hers, a hairsbreadth away.

Oh. Her knees felt like water, the slight bump on her knee all but forgotten. Oh. She felt as if all the oxygen had left her body, reducing her to the most elemental form of herself, full of fire and breath. And desire.

She leaned back slightly and looked directly into his eyes. Passion made her bold and she wanted him to see it in her eyes. "Yes to all of it. *All* of it."

The words barely left her mouth before his lips came down on hers hard. Hot. The heat consumed her. She had never felt this way before. Suddenly, every love song she had ever heard, every romantic movie, every romance novel she had ever read…it all made sense.

Oh. Like that. I get it now, but it's so much more.

His tongue danced with hers hotly, briefly, and she realized…*there are no words for this.* She understood completely at that moment why some people would throw away anything to have this feeling.

She slid her tongue alongside his, tentatively, then more daringly as his low groan told her what she needed to know. He wanted her too. The thought thrilled her to her core. *He wants me too.*

She marveled at the feel of the muscles cording in his back, flexing and bunching under her hands. His hands, in turn, enveloped her in velvety steel strength. Still his mouth slanted hotly over hers, his strong lips shaping and molding hers to his whim. His hands dropped low, tracing her back and lower, over and over. Bay could feel his heartbeat through his flannel shirt. It excited her to know she affected him. *This* affected him.

This was happening. The two of them, this kitchen, and this physical storm...all happening. *And I bought you here.* It stunned her briefly. She knew now she had summoned him, conjured him. Her absent doodling and daydreaming had somehow worked itself into a charm, pulling him viscerally to her side.

He wrapped his arms around him even tighter. He strained even closer, his hips pressing, his breathing ragged. "I want...This feels..."

"I know, yes."

He buried his face in her neck as her body formed against his. "Where's the..."

"Down the hall. Hurry, Declan."

To her surprise, he hauled her up and into his arms, kicking his shoes off as he strode down the hall.

"You have bewitched me, woman." He growled. "Why can I think of nothing but this? Nothing but you? Your skin..." he kissed her throat. "Your mouth..." he kissed her hard on the lips. "And other parts of you...he kicked open the bedroom door. "...that I'm about to discover."

She bounced slightly as she landed on the bed, but only had a second to register that before her his hands were pulling her t-shirt over her head. Only the hall light was on, but it lent the perfect lighting as far as Baylyn was concerned. Just enough.

*Thank God I wore the pink bra...*she thought hazily.

Declan rolled onto his back, bringing her with him, both of them out of breath. In a tangle of arms and legs, they laid together, her head on his chest, his arms around her as he stroked her hair.

"I liked your picture, by the way." His arm was around her, his fingers fluttering around her eyes and hairline, the feeling so sweet it was making her drowsy.

"What picture?" she managed.

"The one of me on the table."

"There's no picture of you on the table." She propped herself up on one elbow, looking down at him.

"Sure there is. It's hand drawn. It looks like you drew it, anyway. There is some doodling and leaves around it. Wait, where are you going?"

Baylyn grabbed a robe from the corner of the bed and whipped it around her, tied it as she was walking down the hall. "I'm getting us some water."

She strode to the table and there, next to the pizza box, was the notebook she was doodling on. Except what she thought were vines and leaves and hearts were actually small parts of the bigger picture, for in the middle, where her mindless doodles connected, a perfect likeness of Declan appeared.

Well, there's another power that was stronger. Summoning. There was no doubt now. She summoned Declan to come to her tonight. Although, all things considered, this certainly couldn't be seen as a bad thing.

She stretched luxuriously, feeling deliciously decadent. Sexy. Powerful. And hungry.

"Declan!" she called. "How many pieces of pizza do you want?"

Chapter 17

"Baylyn, you have to sit down if you want me to put your hair up." Cat drawled as she reached a little unsteadily for her wine glass.

Baylyn grabbed the magazine picture featuring her choice and sat down on the chair in her bedroom. "I wish I had time to get my nails done too."

"Don't worry about it. Your last polish color was too red anyway. What was that called, Summer Slut? It's probably a good thing you didn't have time."

Baylyn laughed. "You are such a bitch. It was called Poppy Daydreams. And look who's talking...you with your Smothered Evening eye shadow."

Cat paused in her deft movements to tug Baylyn's hair a little. "Probably not a good idea to insult me right now."

"Fine." Baylyn grumbled. "You look wonderful, by the way." Cat was wearing a dress a little outside of her comfort zone. She of dark clothes and straight hair and sensible shoes was actually wearing a fitted royal blue dress and low heels.

"It's a pick me up. Things kind of fizzled out with the paranormal guy."

"Ah. His loss, Cat."

"Whatever. Not worth talking about. What are you wearing tonight?"

Cat finished Baylyn's simple yet elegant hairstyle. They had decided on a slight pouf with a casual braid around it, and the final result was chic and classy.

"I thought I'd wear that black dress I wore to that thing a couple months ago."

"Come on, Baylyn. You can do better than that. Go for the glamour, girl! Half the town's going to be at the Whitfield Gala. You know all the women love to dress up and show off."

"Declan's probably not even going to be there, Cat. And seriously, it's the Whitfield Gala. The most exciting thing that happens every year is that Bob Tucker from Tucker Travel gets drunk and tries to hit on Margaret from Sahara Desserts but she's too busy pouting over not winning a door prize to notice."

Baylyn slid on the plain black dress while Cat rooted through the clothes she brought for something dressier.

"Here." She poked Baylyn's arms through a sparkly silver sweater with crystal buttons, and then pulled off the clunky platform shoe Baylyn had put on in order to slide on a sexy black heel. She tossed her some chandelier earrings.

Baylyn sighed. "Oh, for goodness sake. Fine."

They stood side by side and looked in the full length mirror. "You look beautiful." Cat smiled at Baylyn. "All this work you put into this event tonight, it's going to be an amazing night. Wait 'til Declan gets a load of you."

Bay tried to avoid the topic. Declan wouldn't be coming tonight. Despite both of them trying to make some time in their calendars, it seemed impossible in the last two weeks to connect. Even the texts had slowed down. Bay had this gala to plan and it always seemed like something came up with Declan. She had really hoped to spend the evening with him. She needed some downtown after the stress of planning a fundraiser for the literary council, with over 300 people attending. Just the other night, they had planned to talk, but Bay had fallen asleep and missed his phone call. They'd played phone tag since. Two weeks since.

Although she tried to keep it positive, her heart was sending her brain different messages. Fears and self-esteem issues were resurfacing-feelings that she was sure she had corralled and catalogued exactly where they needed to be: in the past. It was disheartening to see how quickly they were surfacing when the slightest doubt came into play.

Baylyn frowned. She shared her doubts with Cat, who wore a look of irritation as Bay spoke.

"Plus, he's got some other business thing, I guess. You know his company bought a table though." Baylyn paused. "He hasn't really...I haven't heard much from him lately. He's called off a couple of dates, too."

Cat checked her lipstick. "Again? Did he say why?"

"Well, once it was something about a missing permit, preventing work on a construction site. The next time it was some emergency meeting about malfunctioning equipment. This last time, he just sounded...frustrated and tired. You don't think maybe there's someone else, do you? That maybe he wasn't tired. Maybe sounding guilty of something? This is exactly what happened with Rob."

Cat shook her head. "No, I don't think that's it. Have faith, Bay. He's a good guy. Maybe things will calm down now that this event is almost over."

Baylyn bit her lip nervously. Tonight, Declan's mother and brother would be sitting at Table 11. He had talked his mother into filling the two tables his company had sponsored for the Whitfield Library. He had yet to introduce her to his family, so she felt it would be awkward going over to introduce herself. Maybe the best thing would be to wait until Declan could introduce them. This would have to wait, because something suddenly came up with Declan.

Again.

Instead, she'd sit at her library's table, with the same people she knew and loved, and it would be a comfortable night. So disappointingly comfortable.

The banquet hall was lavishly decorated and the low lighting was perfect to accentuate the glitter and crystals everyone seemed to be wearing. Convenient that at the same time the lighting flattered every single woman there.

Once there, Cat and Baylyn split up and wandered around, greeting guests, shaking hands and hoping to open pocketbooks and wallets on the silent auction. Baylyn, as a co-chair, was determined to beat last year's fundraising total. This gala was paramount to additional funding for her livelihood.

She had smiled and spoken with most of the guests, and she was truly ready for the night to be over with. Her black heels she wore looked amazing, but all Bay could think about was her pink fuzzy slippers, waiting for her at home. People were here, looking over the auction items, and at this point the evening could truly run itself. She thought about ducking out but was unable to do so. Half an hour later people began finding their seats.

Including Declan.

Her heart actually skipped a beat when she saw him.

Declan? What was he doing here?

Chapter 18

The master of ceremonies began speaking, and the already dim room got even dimmer. Conversation hushed as the Mayor began his yearly introductory speech. There were so many tables this year she could barely make her way to her table after introducing the speaker.

She still hadn't spoken with Declan. She tried to make her way over to him, but the crowds were moving in her direction. He waved to her and blew her a kiss. She was excited yet puzzled to see him. Just as she had the thought her phone alerted her to a text. It was Declan.

Declan: crisis averted.
Baylyn: all OK?
Declan: now that I'm here, yes. You look amazing.
Bay: and you look super handsome.
Declan: talk after speaker? Later?
Bay: can't wait.

She looked up and nodded at him as the speaker droned on. When she was securing a speaker for tonight's activities, she had a vague feeling she had ignored about not asking him to speak and now she remembered why. *Captain Longwinded.*

There was a man sitting next to Declan that not only had to be his brother, but could even pass as his twin. That must be the infamous brother, Devin, back from the out of town trip Declan told her about. In the olden days, they would have politely described him as a rakish playboy.

She nudged Cat. "I think that guy sitting next to Declan is Devin, his brother. They really resemble each other."

Cat snorted. "Look at him. Hellooooo, formal event? Is it too much of a hassle to put a tie around your neck? Brush your hair?" The man in question, noticing the attention, lifted his drink in a mock salute. Cat gave a little shudder. "No, *thanks.*"

Bay couldn't take it anymore. The mayor made no indication that he was ready to stop. The waitresses had the salad plates ready to serve. She leaned down as if she was getting something out of her purse and created a quick spell quietly under her breath. Harmless, really. The mayor wrapped up his sentence, looked up with a puzzled look on his face and announced his speech was done. He received a standing ovation. *Probably in gratitude,* thought Baylyn ungraciously.

Although she tried to not use her magic in public, who knows how long he would have gone on. Besides, she needed to talk to Declan and find out why his plans had changed. It always seemed to be something, but then he was always so glad to see her.

The first course was placed before them by bustling staff; they had the requisite tossed salad with dressing and rolls with butter. A lovely stuffed chicken breast with mashed potatoes and gravy, as well as asparagus and baby carrots on the side were to be the entrée, Cat's addition to the planning.

Now that it wouldn't be rude to do so, Declan made his way over to her table. Baylyn watched him striding toward her, once again breathless and entranced at the figure he cut—cool, confident, and oh, so sexy. *And he's mine,* a little voice said.

He crouched down by her seat.

"You're here!" Baylyn exclaimed delightedly.

"And you're beautiful. I'd ask you to join us but it looks like my mother was able to strong-arm all of her bridge partners to come. Devin's going nuts with all the hen talk."

She laughed softly. "Poor guy. Maybe he should have worn ear plugs."

"What?" Declan motioned to his ears. 'I can't hear you, my earplugs and everything".

"Oh, you. Funny guy."

"Do you want to go get a drink?"

Baylyn gestured to her already full glass. "I just got one, and…" she nodded in the direction of Declan's table…"it looks like your mother wants you back at the table."

Declan sighed tiredly before turning and giving his mother a short wave. "Mother calls. But save me a dance, will you?" He gently drew her hand up to his mouth and kissed it softly, then delivered a soft, scruffy kiss to her cheek. His breath was hot on her cheek and he whispered in her ear. The women at Baylyn's table nearly sighed with the romance of it all. They were in the library often enough to see Baylyn and her "fine young man."

"Count on it." beamed Baylyn.

Declan gave a charming little half bow. "Ladies." He strode back to his table.

Baylyn held that final scorching look he had given her in her memory for a long moment before fluttering back to earth. Good thing he didn't try to hold both hands as her other hand was cramped from hanging onto her seat to prevent any unwanted levitation.

Dinner went without a hitch and people were free to move about and socialize and hopefully, drive up the bids on all the silent auction prizes. Baylyn and Declan were looking over the door prizes: A hot stone massage here, a round of golf there, even a complete set of Harry Potter hardcover books. Her arm was tucked into hers as they walked.

"I was thrilled to meet your mother. She seems so nice." They had ambled over to her table and Declan had introduced her.

He squeezed her to him. "I'd like to think so. I'll guess I'll keep her. Care for another drink?"

Baylyn nodded happily at him. "Tonic water, with a twist of lime. Lots of ice, like the last one. I have too much to watch over to drink."

"No need to explain." He gave her arm a gentle, warm squeeze. "Be right back."

Cat, looking both ways, hurried across the room to Baylyn. She looked slightly tousled and also mad enough to spit nails. "Just ran into the brother outside!" she spat.

"Devin? You met? I take it that it didn't go well?"

"I'd say. He's a pig. I went out onto the patio to get some fresh air, and Brutus over there practically ran me over showing one of the other Neanderthals running a football play. I fell down. Almost."

"Cat, you know he didn't mean it."

"I told him he should have been paying more attention and he told me I needed to 'loosen up and chill out'. He actually tried to pull the clip out of my hair, told me I was acting like an uptight shrew with a stick up my ass. That ape needs some manners. Ooooooh!" She sighed loudly. "At least you look happier. Where is Declan, by the way? Did you find out why he was able to come?"

"He's getting me a drink and holy hell, who is *that?*"

Sex in a red dress. That is what that is. Baylyn watched the blonde woman walk in. *Everyone* watched the woman walk in. Wait, that wasn't walking, that was slinking. The shoes were silver sparkling platform heels. The legs, long and lean, the dress slit up to here. Baylyn's eyes continued up the woman's body as she sashayed over to the bar like she was on a mission.

She had a tiny waist, which only accentuated her enormous boobs. Completing the whole Jessica Rabbit picture was a stylish messy bun, gold glittering jewelry and perfect makeup.

She was absolutely beautiful, she knew it, and she was heading straight for Declan.

Shit. Certainly every woman in the place was feeling a little inferior at this moment but no one more so than Baylyn right now. Why hadn't she listened to Cat and put on something a little slinkier? A little more glamorous? A little more anything? She tugged on her hem a little.

This "sex in a red dress" made her way over to Declan.

He did not seem surprised to see her. Just the opposite.

As color rose in Baylyn's cheeks, she watched Red as she leaned up to whisper in his ear. She leaned back, then placed a manicured hand on Declan's chest and tossed her head back, laughing.

Apprehension slid cold fingers down Baylyn's back. *Who was that?* She watched as Declan stepped back from the bar, holding two drinks. Bay's drink and Declan's drink. She watched in shock as he offered her drink to Red. Her drink. Red took it gracefully and to Baylyn's surprise, turned with Declan and made her way to Declan's table, where she greeted his mother like a long lost friend.

Cat, who also had joined the rest of the room in goggling at Red, turned to Baylyn.

"That right there...now, that doesn't look good."

Baylyn mumbled to Cat, "Maybe she's a cousin?" Even as she said the words they fell flat. Declan sat down right next to the blonde, an inscrutable expression on his face.

Declan did not have ESP. He did not have telepathy. He did, however, get gut feelings, and right now, his gut was standing and banging a gong. He felt rather than saw everyone turn to look at a new arrival.

Before he even turned around, he knew it was Crystal. And in that moment, he wished he had the gift of telekinesis. Maybe even the ability to teleport.

Crystal, bathed in a wave of some overbearing spicy cologne, breezed up to him at the bar.

"Darling." She said, silkily.

He looked at her dispassionately. "Crystal. And it's not darling, it's Declan."

She waved a hand. "Semantics. Here I am. Couldn't wait to see you. Me and you, just like old times. Unless… unless your date pulled her nose from a book to come tonight?"

"Baylyn has more kindness and charm in her little finger than you and your personal shopper combined."

He gritted his teeth as she threw her head back and laughed a little too brightly at the insult.

"I'll be saying hello to your mother. She's the one who invited me, after all. She tells me I'm at your table. Right next to you." *Oh, I don't think so,* thought Declan. *This ends all ways of bad and what is wrong with my mother?*

He spared a glance at Baylyn, hoping she hadn't witnessed that.
Of course, she had. And Cat, the Ethel to her Lucy, had as well.
One fire at a time, he thought.

Some of the other women at his mother's table were up wandering around, so Declan sat for a moment, trying to get his mother's attention. He endured the gaggle of women at his table air kissing, and Devin's smirk, and shot a warning glance at his mother, mouthing, "We need to talk." His mom raised her glass to him, a confused look upon her face. It was obvious that she thought she had done a good deed but now doubted herself.

Crystal touched his arm again and leaned into him. Declan turned right then, aligning their mouths near each other as Crystal said "Now this is fun."

Excusing himself, he made a beeline for Baylyn's table where she had already risen. "Declan, be right back. Powder room." She hadn't met his gaze. This wasn't good. After shooting him one last hurt look, she scurried away, Cat in her wake.

The door closed on the ladies room. Cat did a quick reconnaissance and scanned for feet under the stalls. After making sure they were alone in the ladies' room, Baylyn stared at Cat. "Who the hell is that blond tramp? I am so not feeling good about this."

She paced. Cat offered helpfully, "You should probably check your teeth. Asparagus does you no favors."

Baylyn groaned and furiously rinsed her mouth. "Dammit, why didn't you tell me that before?" She picked out the offending particle and hurled the green speck into the sink.

"Oh, so sexy. I bet Blondie doesn't get food in her teeth." She fished a mint out of her purse and threw it in her mouth.

"Stop it." Cat grabbed Baylyn's shoulders and turned her back toward the mirror. "She isn't one tenth the woman you are. Have some faith in yourself! I can't believe I'm saying this, but have some faith in Declan. He's not Rob. And you've changed, too. You're smarter, kinder, and wiser since him. Not to mention you're still absolutely gorgeous! Look!"

"Yes, look. Look at me, Cat. Yeah, I'm dressed for our library event, but she's...*dressed for a whole different kind of excitement.*"

Slumping on the chaise in the corner of the restroom, Bay tried to swallow the burning lump in her throat. "Malfunctioning backhoe, my ass."

Seizing his chance to find out what agenda Crystal really had up her sleeve (or lack thereof), Declan stormed back to the table where she was sitting. "What, may I ask, are you doing here?"

Crystal pouted prettily. "Well, you wouldn't return my phone calls, and of course I had to return your coat. It was so nice of you to lend it to me. It was so cold that night, after all." She shivered at the memory, drawing even more male glances.

Declan remembered that night so long ago a little differently, as he had lent her that coat to cover up the obscene amount of skin and cleavage she was showing in the top that barely covered her breasts.

Crystal kept up her chatter. "So since you never returned my phone calls, I figured I'd drop it at your mother's, so I just popped on over. Your mother was such a dear and asked me in for a bit, she seemed to think we were still a couple."

Declan was seething. "I don't discuss my dating life with my mother, Crystal. We've been done for months, anyway."

Where was Baylyn?

As if he hadn't spoken, Crystal continued. "...and she was telling me about the Gala, and I couldn't turn her kind invitation down, and she thought we could just be catching up here. Then I saw you at the library the other day, and I saw exactly what your mother was talking about. She had said you were stressed from work and not having a lot of fun. It took me a little bit of time to understand, but now I know why you were so sharp with me. It's because you're so tired. And, like your mother said, you must miss me and the social life you had."

Declan sat down next to her wearily. "Crystal. Crystal. I haven't returned your phone calls or texts because we're not dating anymore." He took her hands in his as he turned to face her, shaking her hands gently on the "not dating anymore" part.

"I care about you, wish you well and all that, but there was no need to drop by the house." *I'd rather you had given that coat to the homeless shelter than track me down like the bloodhound you are. You could have saved yourself a trip.*

Crystal appeared sheepish, and surprisingly, genuine. "I know. I just miss our...time together." Her eyes were teary as she reached to give him an awkward hug. Her hands remained on his lapels and she sighed. She pulled his head down and rested her forehead against his. "I miss you so much, Declan. We are meant to be together."

Faker, he thought.

Declan leaned back, a rueful smile on his face. "Cubic Zirconia."

"What?"

He tipped Crystal's chin up and said, "Your tears. They sparkle like diamonds, but they're still fake, dear." He used his thumb to wipe off a tear.

Declan's eyes cut over to Baylyn's table...still not there...but oh, no. There she was standing there in the hall, her beautiful, big blue eyes taking in the entire scene of the fake hug, fake tears, and even more fake Crystal.

Baylyn blinked, shook her head sadly, and turned to leave. She passed the bar as she left, not even noticing Reynaud sitting at the bar, ensuring that Crystal did and said exactly what he wanted her to.

Looks liked my mission was accomplished, he thought happily. *Right on schedule.*

"It's been a week, Bay." Baylyn dodged Cat, who was stubbornly standing in front of her, eyes blazing, arms crossed. Cat wouldn't let her get to the circulation desk.

"There's got to be some mistake, Baylyn. I am a total skeptic and even I think there's got to be a reasonable explanation for this thing you saw." She waved her hands in the air.

Bay gave a quiet shriek. She finally feinted one way and ducked another, out of Cat's way. "Don't talk to me about that party. Ever, Cat. I don't want to discuss it."

"Baylyn." Cat followed her patiently. It doesn't even make sense. You guys have been dating. Pretty damn seriously. He's told you he has actual, real feelings for you, Baylyn, and you have feelings for him. Even now, after this. I dare you to tell me you don't."

"Yes, I do. Did. I mean, I do. Of course I do. But I wish you could have seen his reaction when he saw me watch them kiss, or almost kiss, or hug, or whatever the hell was happening between the two last week. That was something, Cat, don't tell me it wasn't."

Baylyn was seething with frustration, even a week later. Even the air around her was shimmering with electricity. *Settle down. Wouldn't do to let loose with any kind of magic right now,* she thought, looking at the library patron with her three little boys, standing up at the counter waiting to check out books.

Baylyn made a move toward the counter again but Cat intercepted her. "I'll get this one. Go take a break. Go have some tea or something, really. It will make you feel better. I had a cup earlier and it made me feel so much better."

Baylyn looked around the library. It was clean, quiet, and tidy. No one would miss her if she hid in the back for a few minutes.

Baylyn sighed and loosened her every constant tight shoulders. She nodded wearily. "I'll just take a few moments."

"Take as long as you need. We'll be fine up here."

Baylyn sat sullenly in a comfortable chair in the back room of the library and held a steaming cup of tea. She absently bobbed the tea diffuser up and down, letting it steep. The tea wasn't so much of a draw for her as the fact that she could, just for a moment, still her thinking. Unfortunately, it wasn't working.

Her brain churned as she sadistically replayed the same party scene over and over. She closed her eyes and put her head back on the puffed comfortable headrest of the chair, aware that tears had leaked out of the corners of her eyes and were running down her face.

She wished she could spell her pain away.

All she could think of was how could she have misjudged him so badly?

She rehashed an earlier conversation with her best friend. "But you can't give up just like that over Declan. Baylyn, he comes around here all the time. The man trips over his feet looking all googly eyed at you. From what I hear, your dates get better and better and better." Cat reached out and held both of Bay's hands. "Can you deny that? That you're just as lost over him as he is over you? That's why I'm telling you, there's some reasonable explanation for this."

Pushing herself out of the chair, she reached for her light jacket and scarf, and then walked to the front where Cat was checking out books. "I need to leave for a minute. Maybe walk around and clear my head. Moping's over. It needs to be over. You got this?"

Cat smiled a sad smile. "I got this."

Baylyn paused to hug Cat tightly on her way out of the back. "Thank you for being my friend, Cat. Even without saying anything, you always help me see things a little more clearly."

Chapter 19

It's for the best. It's for the best.

Baylyn repeated that phrase over and over until to her ears, the words sounded nonsensical. She was currently scrubbing the legs of her kitchen table, ready to attack the spindles on the kitchen chairs next. Ordinarily, she would have dance music on—something from her iPod, where she had a playlist entitled simply "dance". It energized her and kept her moving fast, whether she was out jogging, shelving books or home like today…scrubbing the sink, vacuuming, or making the bed.

The trick or treaters had come and gone and she had blown the candle out on her small carved pumpkin.

As was her habit when she was upset, she was cleaning the house. It would be far easier to use a few spells to tidy up, but Bay felt she needed the physical work to keep her mind off things.

Theo hadn't left her alone, certain that since Baylyn was sitting on the floor, it was obviously to pet and worship her. She purred incessantly, weaving and rubbing the chair legs, climbing up and over Baylyn.

"I want nothing more to think about than naps in the sun and kibble." Baylyn said to her companion, scratching her under the chin. The cat purred and hummed, obviously delighted at the attention.

"Your biggest worry is...what? You certainly don't have to worry about boy cats coming along and breaking your heart. It's easier that way, Theo. Don't ever forget it."

Oh sure, he had come into the library to smooth things over, to "explain" himself. And ok, sure he looked sorry. Truth be told, she had to physically restrain herself by holding the counter to avoid flying into his arms the first time he had come in following the debacle of a party to beg for an explanation.

She had told him that night in no uncertain terms, "do not come after me." She had missed too many signs in her past relationship of deception and this time, the signs were making themselves clear.

Crystal clear, one could say.

And to his credit, there was only that one time at the library where he came in to make his case. He persisted, though, calling several times and leaving voicemails. She didn't return his calls and once she heard his voice on voicemail, she deleted it without listening to the rest. Funny how he was able to leave messages and send texts now.

But today? Today was a bad day. She was turning the big 3-0. Single and alone.

Thinking that this would be one birthday to remember, and she'd have people to remember it with, she'd ordered a sinfully rich chocolate cake from the bakery. Calories didn't matter on your birthday, she had always rationalized.

She had tried to cancel the order after their falling out with no luck, so she found herself walking into the bakery with all intentions of picking up the cake. To eat it alone. By herself.

Probably not even using a plate.

A sad, single candle signaling the end of her twenties and a despondent foreshadowing of the loneliness to come.

She knew she was being a sad sack about it. She thought of it as she waited in the deep line. Couldn't every girl throw themselves a pity party now and then? And what good was a party without a good healthy dose of some heart healthy chocolate?

She moved forward in line, still four away from the counter. The lady in front of her was talking on the phone with someone, and she was naming all of the cupcakes available that day. *Lemon crème, bacon maple, chocolate pudding...*

Bay stood, letting her mind wander. What was that phrase about pudding? Proof was in the pudding. The proof had been in the pudding in this case. Talk about your apt phrases. Canceled dates.

Promises to call, then nothing. The repentant flowers and promises it wouldn't happen again, only to happen the very next night. Unreturned phone calls and his over the top attention to the gorgeous blonde, who obviously knew him far too well. Proof was right.

Damn him.

Her chocolate craving gone and without even picking up her birthday order, Baylyn turned around and walked out, barely seeing anything in front of her.

Just like that. This was supposed to be a special, magic filled birthday. Not only had she planned on celebrating it with her wonderful friends, but Declan, too. When she had received her annual Happy Birthday call and song from her mother early in the morning, Elise spoke again of the huge changes Bay was in store for. As if she needed a reminder that this was the birthday to end all birthdays in the ways of power. For on this day, at the moment of her birth on the thirtieth year, she would come into her full power. Her mother reminisced about how she had felt—the full power that came from *her* mother, her *mother's* mother and further back than Bay could imagine. No more lightweight, simple spells.

Everything changed today.

As she got in her car to head home, she sat for a moment. Great, heaving sobs came out, wracking her body until she was slumped over the wheel, exhausted. She finally sat back and worked a spell for her car to drive itself home, because she certainly didn't trust herself behind the wheel.

And now, the cake forgotten, she was on her hands and knees scrubbing the underside—the *underside*—of a kitchen table. Who would ever notice the underside of a kitchen table, never mind the fact that it was clean?

Finishing, she gave it a few more swipes with a dry cloth, then rinsed and put away the bucket and wood soap. She fed the cat who now sat curled at her feet while she nursed a strong cup of tea. Somehow, filling the tea kettle and setting it on the stove to boil made her feel better.

For a few minutes, she sipped the hot, sweet tea and stared into space, her thoughts a confused jumble and her emotions running wild. The whole time she was unaware that tears were slipping down her cheeks onto her spotless table.

"Enough is enough, Theo. I've cleaned everything I can and gone for a run. Might as well see what I can do at the library—I'll get something done now since it's closed."

The moment Baylyn got up, the cat weaved through the chair legs again and at the "library", her cat's weaving increased in speed and velocity until she went and stood by the carrier. "You're a smart little thing, aren't you? First, I better shower."

Half hour later, barefaced and damp haired, she drove to the library, her cat in tow. She had all those boxed documents she could organize in the basement storage area. The work would serve two purposes for her. She couldn't work in the basement during library hours because of the patrons. Second, and more importantly, it would help take her mind off Declan, at least for a little while.

Ordinarily she would enjoy this weather. Tonight, though, it gave her the shivers. She felt cold to her bones. It was getting on to the better part of this Saturday evening and already it was thoroughly dark outside, with stark branches trembling in a slight breeze and the occasional nippy gust. Seemed like a cooler Halloween night than in the past.

She unlocked the library, flipped on a few minimal lights, and let the cat out of her carrier. Theo murmured an appreciate meow as she darted off, most likely in search of the elusive scanner's light at the circulation desk.

She locked the library doors behind her. She didn't want any patrons seeing the lights on and attempt to come in and borrow materials or trick or treating. She made her way to her least favorite place in the library, the basement. Baylyn disliked the feeling she got when she was down there alone, especially in the past six months or so. Only a small portion of the basement was open to the patrons. The rest served as storage for books in repair, stacks of books waiting for the book sale and paper records. Just like most old basements in Whitfield, there was little natural light and there always tended to be a damp smell despite the new carpet and fresh paint.

Plus, there were all those weird noises she had heard from the basement. She and Cat had checked it out on numerous occasions and she had also mentioned it to Declan when he was looking up old town history on the microfiche. He had heard the noises too, but like Baylyn, was unable to determine what they were, or where they were coming from.

Yes, it had been a week, and the sadness was finally waning. Unfortunately, the anger was starting to increase. She wasn't sure if she was angrier with herself or with Declan. A fresh wave of grief swept over Baylyn as she stood in the exact spot she had stood with Declan. Right here was where he smiled at her tenderly and reached out his hand to caress her cheek before leaning in closer for a kiss…

Why are you doing this to yourself? She brushed back bitter tears and tried to swallow past the lump in her throat. *Focus on the task at hand.*

"Baylyn! Baylyn! Where are you? I know you're here, Birthday Girl!"

Cat's voice echoed throughout the empty space, and the large bakery box shielded her face as she came down the stairs.

"Surprise!"

"But how did you…"

"Sue from the bakery called me when you didn't return her call or pick up your order, so I picked it up, and was going to bring it over to your house but it was dark…" she set the box down on the table and smiled. "…and I knew where you'd be."

"How'd you get in?" Baylyn looked from the bakery box to Cat.

"I have keys, you know."

Baylyn tearfully squeezed her friend in a grateful hug. "Thank you for doing that. This. Thank you for being my friend and mostly ignoring me for my own good."

"Let's get this bitch upstairs and get a couple of forks, Baylyn. I have had to smell this all the way over here. Chocolate cures all. Well, makes it tolerable at least. And girl—you need some chocolate."

"Why, Cat, I believe you're right. Lead the way."

Chapter 20

The cake did smell delicious. Baylyn started following Cat up out of the basement, and then paused when she felt something. A frisson of fear? Awareness? Premonition? Whatever it was, icy chills went up and down her back. She felt she was being watched; a feeling she had before, several times, but tonight, she felt even more so. Perhaps next weekend she'd perform a cleansing ritual down in the space.

I'll have Cat come down with me in a bit, dispel some of these nerves. I'm sure it's nothing.

Rubbing her arms, she went upstairs to become the other half of a two person birthday celebration.

After many forkfuls of cake had been sampled, they sat back in their chairs, sated.

Baylyn leaned back and patted her stomach. "I haven't needed a tissue in over an hour."

"That's because chocolate helps a stuffy nose. It helps a skinned knee, too. It also helps heal a headache, a bad day, and a breakup."

At the word, Baylyn looked down as her smile faded.

"You'll figure it out, Baylyn. Once your emotions settle down, and you can actually hear what he's got to say..." Bay shook her head.

Cat continued. "No, now listen. You've been my voice of reason for years. If you hadn't been with me through my whole breakup with Bud, I don't know what I would have done. You saved me. Now he was the epitome of a horrible person. And when you found out about Rob, we both agreed he was also a terrible person. But Bay, that's not what kind of man I see in Declan. I think you know it, too."

A quiet silence filled the space. The clock ticked the seconds away.

It was Cat who broke it. "We're not to blame for those two idiots, either. None of what happened to me or you was our fault. It's taken me a long time to not see Bud in every man I meet or to read too much into body language or tone of a text."

"Or no text?"

"Stop." Cat swiped some frosting on her finger. She shook it at Bay. "You see him cheating on you because that's what you wished you had known Rob was doing behind your back." She licked the frosting off. "It doesn't mean that's what it was. You looked at his face and saw guilt. I looked at him and saw only desperation—not guilt, passion or even interest. I've seen how he looks at you. I only wish that someone would look at me the way he looked at you."

Baylyn gave her a watery smile. "He does have a brother. He's very handsome. Remember him? He semi-tackled you and complimented you on your uptight ass."

Cat sniffed, nose in the air. "Oh, please. He looked like a total playboy. My guy? He'd have to be a neat freak like me. And old enough to be a real man. I want a family someday, and I don't want to be the mother to a baby and my man. He's going to have to hold up his end of the bargain and be a committed partner and co parent, not be messing around anymore with *sports* and football games and his *buddies*."

Cat opened her mouth to respond but just then, there was a stealthy scraping sound. This time, there was no mistaking that it was coming from the basement. They both cocked their heads to listen and heard it again. *Scraaaaaape*...Someone or something was in the basement...and they were doing their damndest not to be heard.

She looked at Baylyn with wide eyes and mouthed, "Did you hear that?" which was almost unnecessary, because one look at Baylyn and she knew she wasn't the only one to hear the sound. It was no cat. It was no draft. It was no mouse, either. Whatever was down there was big and it was moving around.

Baylyn stood quietly, gathering her long dark hair into a loose tail. Cat shot her a questioning look and Baylyn nodded slowly, seriously. For once and for all, they were going down there to figure out just what was making all that noise. Bay grabbed the emergency flashlight, and Cat grabbed her.

Reynaud winced as he heard the shriek of the old delivery door opening. He instantly spelled it to open without any further noise. He scrambled through it as he had many, many times before to gain access into the library's basement. He never looked at it as breaking and entering…more like borrowing. It's just that he was borrowing when the library was closed. Borrowing the space, if you were. Fewer people that way.

He slid the door shut, and then leisurely ambled over to "his" area, where he had spent several undiscovered hours poring over copies of Declan's filed permits, studying which ones were important and would cause the most delay if they were removed. Once in a while he glanced at his phone, which relayed almost every movement Baylyn made in the library, courtesy of hidden cameras here and there, which he had an "app" for on his phone. Easy enough to install when you could come and go as you please.

Gotta love technology.

Speaking of pleasing, a cup of coffee and things would be perfect.

He closed his eyes, snapped his fingers, and instantly a piping hot cup of perfectly creamed and sugared coffee appeared in his other hand.

The two women looked at each other as another squeak was heard. Baylyn, jaw set, headed toward the stairs to investigate, fearless, but Cat held back, hesitating. "You sure about this? We should call someone, Baylyn. I mean, I have every faith in you—but…well, I just don't want to get in over our heads here."

Baylyn paused and shot her a look. "We've been using these stairs, and that basement, forever. I'm sure whatever's down there is a raccoon or mouse or maybe even another cat, Cat."

She gently jostled Cat's arm and attempted a little humor. "You see what I did there? I said cat, Cat."

Another sound, louder, captured the women's attention.

Cat leaned close to hiss at Baylyn, "You are really a laugh riot, Baylyn. A laugh rye-ott. Fine. Let's go look."

Cat followed inches behind Baylyn until they reached the bottom of the stairs, when suddenly the lights went out and complete, inky darkness surrounded them.

Cat gave a little shriek and turned to run back upstairs. Baylyn grabbed her arm decisively and snapped the light switch. Nothing happened. She toggled the switch on and off a few more times, then with a muttered, "Oh, heaven's sake." She gave a little snap of her fingers and the lights came on.

"Come on." ordered Baylyn. Cat followed dutifully behind her. "It's got to be some animal down here. It's so distracting." As Baylyn advanced further into the room, a feeling of dread came over her. Immediately, she put a protective spell over her and Cat. Wait. She mentally probed the air around her. Something wasn't right. She couldn't feel the comforting weight of the protection spell settle on her shoulders like a comfortable shawl; in fact, she got the equivalent to a bounce back.

She spelled for protection again as Cat came up beside her, but again felt the spell push back against her. What the hell? Even as she finished that thought, dread stole over her again.

A man slinked around the corner of the library stack. Bay grabbed her flashlight in defense and pushed herself in front of Cat. She wished she had called the cops. *He was a weasel for sure, but this was no animal.*

Chapter 21

"You!"

"That's right, me." Reynaud slithered from the shadows.

"How did you get down here? You're not supposed to be down here. You're not supposed to be here at all. How...how did you even get in?"

"He's using the old delivery door, Baylyn."

"Clever girl." he drawled. "Got it in one."

"But why?" Baylyn asked the question at the same time she pushed one more time for her protection spell.

He sardonically arched one dark brow at her. "That's not going to work, love." She gave Cat a quick, hidden look and mouthed, *Call 9-1-1.*

Cat sidled in further back of Baylyn and tried to be inconspicuous about dialing.

"That's not going to work either, little Cat."

"What did you do to the phones?" she asked, as she shook her cell phone, trying to get it to work.

"Same thing I did to the little protection charm Baylyn's trying to work. They've both been...disabled."

Baylyn rocked back on her heels as the realization hit her like a punch to the gut.

"You're a witch." She breathed, her eyes wide.

"I'm a witch."

Cat's eyes widened. "I can't get the…wait. *What?*"

Declan morosely packed for his trip to the other office in Oregon.

Women. He could grow as old as Methuselah and women would confound him just as much then as they did now. One in particular.

Probably worse, because they then would have centuries of time to figure out how to make their men miserable. Really miserable.

He had done everything right this time—took his time, not rushing headlong into anything when his very first instinct was to grab Baylyn, swoop her up and kiss her all the way to the altar.

He actually listened to his mother this time about taking things slow, and look where that had gotten him. Sitting in a cab he didn't want to ride in, on the way to the airport he didn't want to fly out of, to a state he didn't want to be in, all because she wasn't there.

Baylyn.

He pictured her blue eyes shining up at him. Her full, red lips swollen from his stubble-rough face the last time they had kissed. He had apologized for his scruff, whispering soft healing kisses over the reddened areas, teasing her lightly, enjoying the way she giggled breathily and tried to playfully hold him off. Both of them had been dizzy with the heat they generated, intensity of the *want*.

This was ridiculous. The gala had been a week ago, and Bay had yet to return a single call or text. He couldn't imagine how it looked to her. How could he explain it when there wasn't anything to explain?

Trust. She needed to hear about Crystal from him. He knew his Bay had been burned badly by her ex-boyfriend. It saddened him that he and Bay had started feeling off so strong, and then, especially in the last few weeks, things became strained. He didn't see it right away, but when he totaled the number of times he'd been unable to contact Bay and the times he had to reschedule, the picture of why she was so upset started to form more clearly. Add to that Crystal hanging on him at the benefit, with his arms around hers, and it really was no wonder Baylyn thought the same of him that she did of her cheating ex.

What was weirder yet was that after the whole debacle, his work week this week had gone ridiculously smooth on the job sites. Not a single problem had arisen and they were finally moving forward. It had allowed him to inundate Bay with phone calls and texts, albeit with zero success.

He looked aimlessly outside as he watched the cars pass by and the planes overhead. He would just be gone for two weeks. Maybe when he came back he would have a better time trying to get her to understand.

Two weeks would be too much. He knew in his heart the gap was widening, his chance to get her to understand turning into an insurmountable chasm. He needed to see her. He needed to explain. He needed her to understand.

He needed her.

"Turn around." Declan instructed the cab driver. "Turn around. We have to go back."

"Sir, we're almost to the airport. If you left your toothbrush at home, you could get one at the airport, or at the hotel. You just have to ask."

"I mean, turn around, as in I have to go back home. Now. Do it now."

The cab driver must have picked up on the panic in Declan's voice. "No skin off my nose. You're on your own dime, mister."

The cabbie swung a practiced U turn in the "authorized vehicles only" grassy knoll of the highway.

"It's an emergency, right? Well, we're in an emergency vehicle, then. That's how I always think of it."

"I need to get home fast. I don't care how you do it."

Call after frustrating call to Baylyn went directly to her voice mail. That was not a new development, as she had been studiously avoiding him, but he thought if she noticed that he was calling every two minutes, that might pique her interest and she'd have a harder time rejecting his calls.

After half hour, he finally gave up and began calling Cat, only to be met with more of the same.

His suspicion that something was wrong raised another notch. He started to feel a strong pull to be with her and his sense of urgency increased. He had felt like this their night together. He couldn't help himself. The tug to see her, touch her had been so strong. He felt this way now, but the need was different. It was tainted with fear, Bay's fear, and sent his adrenaline into overdrive. The cabbie suddenly locked eyes with his fare's face. "You don't look so hot."

Although the ride home was only another 45 minutes, it felt endless to Declan. Once home, he threw the fare at the driver and opened the garage long enough to toss his luggage in.

Over and over he called Baylyn, then Cat, and finally Baylyn's mother, who had no idea where her daughter was, but "maybe she went on one of her late night runs, or…" there was no missing the barb in the next suggestion, "Maybe out for a birthday dinner with people who care about her." Unspoken was the fact that Baylyn could possibly still be ignoring him, far more likely than the fact that she'd go out to run at night, in the light rain.

His intuition told him something different, however. He sped to Baylyn's house, only to find it dark. The rain had increased, coming down more steadily now. The potential for Bay's run quickly moved down in possibilities. He ventured out into the downpour, circling the house, knocking on her door and windows with no luck.

Cat's house was dark too, but as he debated knocking there, it occurred to him: the library. Of course.

Tires squealing and slipping on the pavement, he sped off into the night.

Reynaud tossed Baylyn a length of rope. "Tie her up, little Cat here. Wouldn't do to have you…"

He didn't finish because Cat whirled around, panicked, to run back up the stairs, but it was as if she ran full tilt into a brick wall. She fell back on her rump, hard, then cracked her head on the floor and laid there, limp.

"Cat!" Baylyn screamed. *He must have put up a blocking spell! Now what?*

"Oh, yes I did. Indeed, I did." said Reynaud as he knelt down by Cat's inert form and roughly tied her hands in front of her, then placed a piece of duct tape over her mouth. He pulled her over to the wall, and then dropped her there unceremoniously.

Baylyn felt behind her at the invisible yet impenetrable wall. There seemed no way to get out of here. She couldn't afford to panic, yet conversely, this seemed to be the exact *right* time to panic. She had sent off a summoning spell to Declan, drawing unseen intricate patterns on her leg over and over in hopes he could be called. She was trapped in the basement with a lunatic who had just knocked out her best friend, put up an invisible barrier, and let's see, what else…*oh yeah*, he was a witch. A *strong* witch. No, no need to panic at all. It didn't keep her from throwing one spell after another at him. Surely, one of them would work.

"Work all the magic you want, my love. Nothing is going to work. I have planned this," he spread his arms expansively, "perfectly. Your little friend is otherwise occupied. Your 'boyfriend', gone. Some boyfriend. He left, Baylyn, and I'm here. Caught him cheating, did you? Some blonde bimbo. Crystal, was it? Such a shame." His tsk-tsk echoed loudly in the space.

"I think you'll finally be able to give me the chance that you never gave me before. I've been watching you and planning this for such a long time."

He sauntered up to Baylyn; laid one repulsive hand on her arm, watching her expression the entire time. "Your powers and mine, Baylyn. Just think of it. Unstoppable together; just think of it. I thought we could get to know each other a little bit before your powers came to pass. I bided my time until I knew your birthday was near. If it wasn't for that damn meddling man, we would have been together already." He circled around her, a trembling hand lightly touching her hair, then roughly pulled her hair elastic out and gathered a thick handful up, pulling her to him.

Baylyn winced with the pain. "You were stalking me this entire time, weren't you?"

"Stalking. Such an awkward, unfriendly word. You are meant to be mine. You are mine. I saw it. Your mother…"

Bay stiffened. "What about my mother?"

"From the time I saw her, I wanted her. I thought it was fate, you know? And she wanted me. All the looks she gave me…all that help I gave her when your father was gone…oh, she wanted me." Reynaud was pacing back and forth. His hands became more animated the more he talked.

"But then, I watched one day as she scryed your future, young Baylyn. I watched. Enthralled. Entranced. I watched in that crystal ball as you grew and became more beautiful with every day, and I saw that you never, ever ended up with anyone happily. There was no love for you in your future, in any of the many futures your mother looked at for you. Until the last one, and it was me. You and me, together forever."

"No!" Baylyn ground out. "Those were just possibilities. You spied on her? During the very time you claimed to be falling for her? You weren't there for her. You were trying to move in on my family while taking advantage of a young woman. That is what you were doing. You're wrong."

Reynaud jerked the handful of her hair and leaned forward threateningly. "I know what I saw."

Baylyn narrowed her eyes and blinked back the tears that came with the sting from her hair being jerked. "What you saw were all possibilities. But never, Reynaud, never in a thousand years, a thousand futures, will I choose to be with you."

"Well, you won't end up with Declan, I've seen to that." Reynaud loosened his grip on her hair and stroked it. It was all Baylyn could do to not scream.

"What do you mean, you've seen to that?"

Reynaud released her hair. "It doesn't matter. You and I will be married by the stroke of midnight while you're still a minor witch. Yes. Tomorrow, when you turn thirty, you'll already be my wife. As a married couple, it will be my right to use your powers with mine as I see fit." Bay's eyes widened as she processed what he was saying.

One thing made itself very clear. Reynaud thought her birthday was tomorrow. Not today. With a flash of understanding Baylyn knew why her mother had kept two birth certificates for her all these years, one for October 31, her real birthday, and another, a forged one, for November 1. The one she had filed with the Witch's Council. For a witch who was born on October 31 would have been monitored very, very closely.

He crossed his arms, assessing her with those flat shark eyes. "I'll make you happy. Of course, you will make me happy too. It will be your duty to make me happy. You won't want to disappoint me." He trailed a finger down the front of her shirt. He began to smile, a slow smile that stopped at his eyes. He moved his head down and closed his eyes as he breathed her in.

She slapped his hand away, feeling sick. "You're a sick bastard." *If only she could keep him talking.* Her thigh hit the side of the chair as she was pushed hard into it. "Does my mother know you're here?"

Reynaud giggled. The sound sent shivers up her scalp. "Your mother. What a sad woman. She believes I disappeared from your lives many, many years ago. Yet here I am. Waiting for you, just like she foretold. Just as handsome as ever. I used your daddy's magic for this little trip from the past, Baylyn. His time travel spell. Guess what. It works."

Chapter 22

Baylyn went white. "Don't talk about my father. Don't even say his name. You stole his spell then!"

"I believe in preparing for any eventuality, yes."

Reynaud clapped his hands and a short, hooded figure appeared, taking form from the ground up, filling out a gown and then just standing there, features shrouded. A small, scared sound squeaked from the corner. It took Bay a moment to realize it was Cat, her mouth bound by the duct tape. She could see Cat's eyes widening in fear.

"What...who is that?"

"Ah, an important person for us. He's going to marry us, my dear."

Oh, God. Baylyn cast a worried glance at Cat, who was lying helpless on the floor. Her eyes were open and flashing fire.

"Oh, and your precious Declan isn't coming to your rescue tonight, bride. He's got some broken things to deal with."

That brow again, looking like a bushy black caterpillar arching up. It sickened her. A more loathsome sight she had never seen.

"Broken things?"

An almost girlish laugh escaped him. "Broken forklift. Broken backhoe. Broken permit. Broken promises. You name it, it's broken."

Declan, where are you?

Declan sped up to the front of the library, jamming the car into park and ignoring all the "don't you even dare" park here signs. As he neared the entrance, he noticed a light on. She was here. He was pulling a credit card out, ready to jimmy the lock or do whatever it would take when he turned the knob and realized that the door to the library wasn't locked.

Alarm bells that had been pinging in his head were now clanging and jangling loudly. No way on earth would Baylyn had come to the library on a Sunday or forget to lock it if she was alone.

His senses kicked into overdrive. Something was very wrong here—every single prickle on the back of his neck told him so.

Quiet, then.

He sneaked quickly through the upstairs of the library, including the office and even the bathrooms, his alarm growing with every empty space he encountered. Nothing.

"Bay!" he hissed. He drew up short, defenses up, when he heard an answering sound. It was the cat, Theo. She padded over to him and loudly burbled to him in a way he had never heard another cat burble. Baylyn joked once that the cat had not ever made that sound except for when Declan was around.

Well, the cat's here. Baylyn has to be here. He watched as the cat dodged back and forth toward the lower level entrance.

The basement! He swiftly moved to the basement stairs and crept down the carpeted steps. As he neared the bottom of the stairs, he could hear murmuring. Baylyn's voice. Then a man's voice…

He could hear a man's smug voice murmuring to someone, then Baylyn's worried voice.

"How could you? He has a sterling business reputation…he's a generous employer…how could you ruin him like that?"

"Didn't your boyfriend ever wonder what was really happening? Why permits he thought were secure, weren't? Bet he blamed the systematic breakdown of his company on his staff, didn't he. Entitled little rich boy. But of all, I'm most proud of my little pawn. My piece de resistance. Crystal. Oh, she played the part perfectly. Wasn't even aware she was being manipulated."

Baylyn's brain whirled. The times Declan had cancelled dates with Baylyn because of work issues. She had wanted to believe him, right up until she saw Declan holding Crystal at the party. That had tipped her over the edge.

She was so irritated with herself. Declan had been telling the truth the entire time. She thought miserably, it sounded like he was telling the truth about Crystal, too. She wasn't his 'someone else', and she was pursuing him, not the other way around. She saw it so clearly now.

What have I done? I threw it away. I threw our relationship away.

"Declan, I'm so sorry!" she whispered, agonized.

Just then, she heard her kitten's faint burbling sound from upstairs. The kind of sound he only made when Declan was around.

He was here!

Declan was close enough to hear Baylyn's sorrowful words.

Not knowing if the man had weapons, Declan peered around the corner. Didn't look like he had anything, except that was Cat on the floor, slumped against the wall, bound and gagged, and a small hooded figure. It looked like something off an evening crime show.

Time to act.

He loudly stepped into the room where Baylyn and Reynaud were locked in their heated exchange.

"Mind if I join your birthday party, Baylyn? I seem to have lost my invitation. Hope I can still attend."

"Declan! What are you…how did you…" Baylyn's eyes immediately filled with grateful, unshed tears. She jumped up from her seat and moved to run to him but Reynaud stopped her with an upturned palm. She froze in midstep, unable to move.

Reynaud looked completely flabbergasted by the new development for a moment, but recovered his composure quickly enough to say, "No one invited you, Declan. Again, showing up where you're not wanted. Go on, have your little hello. In a few minutes, it's not going to matter."

Declan dismissed Reynaud with a look, strode over to Baylyn, grasped her upper arms and drew her up him. He gave her a questioning look. "Are you okay?"

"I'm so sorry."

"I love you." Declan held her face and gave her a hard, hot kiss.

He moved his body in front of Baylyn, protecting her, and faced Reynaud. "Listen, buddy, I don't know what's going on here, but I'm sure there's a way to work it out without anybody getting hurt."

Suddenly Declan felt himself pulled away from her. The surprise caught him off guard and he let go of Baylyn, only to feel like he was turned around and around, being wound up in what felt like a tight and inescapable spider web. Bay moaned, unable to speak, and she looked as if she were frozen in the spot with shock.

"Always butting in. Not this time, Declan. She's mine. And that man..." he pointed to the tiny robed figure, "is going to ensure we're married. Together, our magical powers will be unstoppable. I mean, my magic will be unstoppable. Baylyn here is just along for the ride."

Reynaud looked at Declan, struggling in the invisible web. "You look confused. Did she not tell you?"

Although Declan's body was frozen, his mouth was not. "The only thing I'm confused about is how someone as crazy as you is not locked up somewhere."

"This is good. This is really, really good. So am I to understand not only did Bay not tell you that she was a witch, but she also didn't tell you that tomorrow, when she turns thirty, she'll become so powerful she could destroy this entire building in one blink?"

Bay took a deep breath and tried once again to speak. Nothing would come out. The more attention Reynaud was giving to Declan, the less he could focus on her, and she was regaining control.

Reynaud came close to Declan. "Of course, she couldn't have told you about our impending marriage, since I couldn't ever seem to get to be with her enough to tell her myself." Declan looked back and forth from Baylyn to Reynaud, and let out a high pitched giggle.

Baylyn closed her eyes, praying for strength and power from not only herself but every single ancestor witch she had descended from. She reached out to pull strength from the earth, from the powers surrounding her. The giant clock upstairs had gonged the 10:00 p.m. hour, what seemed about a half hour ago. It had to be almost 10:30 p.m. Her mother had told her what time of night she was born and the exact time she'd get her powers was that time on her 30th birthday.

At 10:30 p.m.

It began as a slow trickling feeling along the back of her calves, warm, thrilling tendrils moving up towards the back of her thighs. The sensation became stronger, almost an electric pulse. She felt the spell Reynaud had used to freeze her melt away, her new magic abilities stretching into her fingers, her back, her shoulders and up into her heart. Up further and further until she could feel the strong, foreign power spiraling through her and settling in as if it belonged all the while. She welcomed it as it filled her spirit and focused her thinking. Her thoughts had never been clearer. Spells were made known to her, filling her mind with the knowledge of her ancestors. Her fear had dissipated.

Reynaud remained unaware and smiled smugly. "It's time. And you…" He wagged a finger at Baylyn. "I see you thinking over there. I don't care that you've finally tossed off the spell. But don't even try anything on me. I told you already your puny magic wouldn't work on me. Why do you think I chose today for us to become one? You might be beautiful, but you really are so dense. Minor powers. You're just a junior witch." He started pacing again. He walked over to Cat and gave her a little push with his brown leather shoe. "A lot of help you are. Enjoying the show?" Baylyn could hear Cat's angry curses even through the duct tape.

"Your only chance of defeating me is *after* your birthday." He spun and walked quickly to Baylyn. He spoke slowly, as if talking to a young child. "Because you'll get your powers then. You'll be married to me already. I will be able to utilize your powers, and together we'll be amazing. You will love me. You will make me an amazing wife."

Baylyn turned toward Declan, making sure he could see her clearly. She mouthed "Trust me." before turning towards Reynaud. She raised her arms directly toward him and announced clearly, "Like hell I will. And Reynaud? A good husband would remember his wife's birthday. Mark this on your calendar, stupid. My birthday's not tomorrow. It's today."

Baylyn murmured her first full spell with the new powers, one built of the moment and of lessons long ago. Strength and energy coursed through her still, filling her with an exciting awareness of how powerful she had become. Her heart was racing; the thrill of the moment moving through her.

With a casual flick of her wrist, a very surprised Reynaud was thrown against the wall and pinned there. The look on his face was comical as he dangled loosely above a completely shocked and unmoving Cat.

The mysterious hooded character disappeared with a poof, empty robe dropping to the floor.

A much stronger and confident Bay rushed to Declan's side. He looked at her, his face showing confusion, fear and love. "What was that? No, wait. Help Cat." She nodded and hurried over to Cat, who was very alert and very angry.

"Cat, are you ok? Oh my God! Are you hurt?" She waved a hand and the rope and duct tape disappeared.

Cat, like her namesake, sprang to her feet, and then teetered unsteadily. "Whoa. That bastard!" She took a step backward. "Bay, what in the world is going on here?"

Baylyn hugged her fast and hard while Cat eyed Reynaud warily. "Is he..."

"He's not going to do anything until I let him do something."

"But how do you know he won't..."

"Relax, and trust me. I promise I will explain things as best I can in a few minutes. First, though, I need to talk to Declan."

Baylyn didn't know how to start. Declan spoke first. "Aren't you worried about him doing something else?" Declan flexed his wrists and kept looking at the suspended Reynaud.

"Did you see me back there?"

"Yes."

"Then hopefully you can believe me when I say he's no longer a problem." Bay worried a thumbnail, and brushed her bangs out of her eyes. "I'm a witch, Declan. That's what you saw back there. I've been keeping this side of my life from you, and today was an absolute game changer. You know that now. Please don't think I'm weird or spooky—it's just a part of me that I can't change. I don't think I would if I could." Bay looked pleadingly up to Declan, who still remained quiet.

"Tonight I learned Reynaud was sabotaging everything so he could keep us apart. Even Crystal was part of his plan. He played upon my biggest insecurities so that he could be with me. I'm should have trusted you. I should have had more faith in you. I'm so, so sorry. I didn't know how you'd react."

Declan silently held her close, his heart beating fast against her. He said nothing.

"I wanted to tell you."

Declan continued to stay mute as he looked down at her solemnly.

"Say something." she begged.

Chapter 23

Declan reached down and grasped her hands so he was holding both of her small hands in his large ones. "Happy Birthday, Baylyn." He dipped his head and kissed her softly. "I love you. I think I loved you the moment I laid eyes on you in the library."

Baylyn could feel her throat close up painfully with unshed tears. *Remember this moment*, she told herself. *Stay in this moment.*

"I love you too, Declan, so much." Her voice broke on the words.

Declan squeezed her hands. "But I don't know about this." He waved his arms at Reynaud, coming to but still stuck suspended from the air, Cat rubbing her wrists, and Bay, looking more beautiful than ever.

They stood in the quiet, the three of them, processing what had just happened. Declan released a long deep breath.

"So you're a witch."

Bay nodded. "Yep."

"Will you help me understand?"

"Yep."

A smile started to splay across Declan's face. "Cause I have to tell you, Bay that was unbelievable." He pulled her to him. "You're a witch, huh? One more thing for me to love about you."

Cat squealed and hugged first Baylyn, then Declan.

"I'm so happy for you both, I could just…" Suddenly Cat's feet left the floor and to everyone's surprise, especially Cat's, she hovered.

"Baylyn!" she screamed. "What the hell!"

Declan stood there, openmouthed. Without looking at Baylyn, he whispered, "How are you doing that?"

Baylyn threw her hands up in frustration. "I'm not doing that! I don't know what's happening. Cat looked down at her. "What did you do?" She held herself very still for a moment. "What's happening to me?" Her loafered feet started to stomp like a two year old, despite being six inches off the ground.

Baylyn quickly thought back to the spell she threw to strip Reynaud of his powers.

"Ne'er do well, you do not own
The awesome powers you once had known
Spells and charms and all of that
Bequeath your magic to my cat."

Cat rolled her eyes from up high. "That's the dumbest spell I ever heard! To your cat? What would make you say to your cat? What would a cat do with magic powers? That's ridiculous!" Still hovering, Cat started laughing. Right at that moment, Theo walked king-like, down the stairs, still a very non-magical cat.

Declan started laughing. "To your cat? Oh, Bay. The only cat down here was your Cat!"

Cat's eyes widened. "Are you flipping telling me that I have his magic now?" She started saying each word as if it were its own sentence. "Are you flipping KIDDING ME? This is awesome!" She started bouncing against gravity in the small lower level basement, hooting the whole while. To watch the always put-together Cat playing as if in a fun house was almost worth the magical mix-up.

"I was thinking cat as in cat *Theo*, not Cat *friend*. I figured his powers would be somewhere safe, where they couldn't hurt anyone." She gave a little laugh. "Obviously I have some things to learn."

Baylyn turned her attention to Reynaud and let him drop. He was no threat to her now, now that he had been stripped of his powers.

"You bitch. You bitch! Give me back my powers." Reynaud looked very different, now that he wasn't so puffed up with arrogance. "You have no right to take them away from me!"

"Actually, Reynaud, I do. 'Do no harm. Do no evil. Don't meddle with another's' powers. Basic Witchwork 101. Any of that sound familiar? And gosh, your little travel through time? Looks like your age just caught up with you. You aren't so pretty now."

Reynaud took a threatening step toward her but a single step was the furthest he got, as a very large, very strong, very Declan hand planted itself in Reynaud's shirt, grabbing a fistful of material.

"I don't think I need to say this twice. Get out of town. Don't come back." He pulled Reynaud up close to him; they stood nose to nose. "And if I see you around here ever again, I will kill you. That is, after I let my fiancé experiment on you. Maybe she'll let me watch her turn you into a billy goat."

Cat interjected as she floated to the ground. "And she could, too. And now I can too. Should we find out?" Bay knew Cat was a fast learner. This was going to be fun.

Declan gave him a shake. "I know it was you, by the way. Do you know how much money you've cost me? How many man hours I've used fixing equipment you sabotaged?" Shake. "How many business meetings I had to cancel, flights I had to reschedule, contracts that were mysteriously lost by the courier, permits unfiled…" His voice got louder and louder the madder he got.

He let go and pushed Reynaud away. "I could sue you for every penny I lost. Hope you have a good lawyer."

"You don't scare me." Reynaud trembled and his voice shook even as he said the words.

Declan quirked an eyebrow at him and smiled. "You should be scared. You'll have a lot to atone for. And it will be an expensive atonement."

Baylyn murmured to Declan, "Wait til the witches council gets through with him." At the mention of the council, Reynaud paled. "He'll be lucky to still be alive."

"Be on your way, Reynaud. We'll meet again—bet on it."

Baylyn pointed a finger at him. "Why don't you slither out of here the same way you got in, and I'd be quick about it. Or we'll try out that billy goat spell right now."

Cat stomped her foot at Reynaud, who fairly ran toward the old delivery door. She floated after him.

Bay took a deep breath. "Is this whole witch thing going to be a problem for you?"

"I don't understand it, but I'll try. From now on, it's you and me, a team, and I won't stand in your way if you want to do what makes you, you."

"Oh, it's not a 'dance naked in the moonlight' witchcraft kind of thing. I'll do like my mother and her mother before her and help people."

"Whatever it is, just share your life with me. Make me a part of it."

"Declan, you already are. You are my life".

"As you are mine." He leaned closer and took her lips in a kiss that seemed to contain all of his feelings…fright, anger, tenderness, and sweet, aching love, then let her go, stroking her cheek lightly.

She looked up at him and blinked. "Wow."

His dimples came out as he smiled back at her. "*Now* who's got the magic touch?"

Epilogue

Baylyn sighed contentedly. Life was splendid. It had taken a little bit of time, but Declan had come to terms with the fact that she was a witch. Well, he said he had, at least. He was trying so hard and his earnestness was yet another appealing thing about him, adding to what she found was a very long list.

She was sitting at her desk at the library looking over some of the new books the local publisher had sent over, a couple of books that looked promising. Perhaps she'd start reading them tonight? After Declan and she cooked dinner together? She smiled to herself.

She looked so forward to their evenings…sometimes at her house where her cat Theo amused Declan to no end, sometimes his house where Bay could use one Labrador or the other as a pillow in front of the fireplace while she and Declan talked, or drank wine.

Yes, life was splendid. She looked off into the distance, lost in dreamy thought.

Cat's stage whisper broke her reverie as she strode over to Bay's desk. "Hey, Miss I-don't-tell-anyone-even-my-best-friend-I'm-a-witch. I think you better watch what you're doing because you're putting on a magic show right now and you don't want any of our little patrons talking, now do you?"

Bay looked at her, confused. "What?"

"You're turning the pages. Except you're not turning the pages."

"Yikes. Thanks Cat. And by the way, speaking of unintentional magic, you might work a little harder at staying on the floor. You seem to have a slight gravity problem today."

"What?" Cat peered down at her feet, which were about three inches off the ground. She gasped.

"You'll learn. Like I had to." Baylyn smiled at her best friend. "Floor, Cat."

The Adventure Continues...

Cat, Charmed

Her water was cooling, and she used her toes to pull the plug. She lay in the tub as all the water drained, standing only when it was gone to rinse the bubbles off with fresh, hot water. Her toes and fingers pruned, she stepped out and wrapped herself in a towel. She took out her favorite lotion and rubbed it onto her entire body, hoping the soft scent of the lotion would help keep her relaxed.

Throwing some blackhead strips on her nose, old yoga pants and a t-shirt, she padded into her bedroom, flopped herself on the bed and grabbed her phone.

Devin: Thinking about you.

Devin: My bookshelves need a prim and proper straightening. You game?

He had teased her mercilessly about being prim and proper when they'd been together. Brazenly, she had told him she'd show him prim and proper. She should be so embarrassed. Instead, a hot flush covered her body. She had controlled the evening, and it felt amazing.

Devin: Hey.

Devin: What time are you home?

Devin: Want to see you.

She rolled over onto her back and held the phone up above her face with two hands. Want to see you? A warm frizzle of excitement ran through her. That sounded promising. She rolled back over and texted back.

Cat: I'm home now.

His response came almost immediately.

Devin: What you doing?

Cat: Waiting for you to want to see me.

There was a pause, probably only a minute or so, where Cat wished there was a recall button. Why would she say something like that? What kind of girl was she turning into?

Devin: Oh, I want to see you. All of you.

Her insides felt as if she had swigged liquor, warm pooling in places newly awakened. Her phone pinged another message.

Devin: What are you wearing?

She looked down at her comfies and typed.

Cat: Silk pajamas, matching undies. Just took a hot bath.

Devin: What color?

Cat: What color do you wish they were?

Devin: You're killing me. I can imagine they feel sexy.

Cat: Come on over and feel it yourself.

Devin: I've been in your driveway. Open the door.

Cat sat straight up. Her hair pins had started falling out as she had rolled around on the bed. Her yoga pants had crept up; her thick socks had pulled down, making her feet look twenty inches long. She heard his soft knock on the door.

Oh, crap.

Silk pajamas? Not even close. This is what happened to dishonest people, she thought, as she ran into the bathroom, yanking the blackhead strips from her nose, wincing in pain. She grabbed her robe, cupped her hand and smelled her breath.

Oh, yes, so sexy, she thought, running downstairs. She hoped Devin could take a joke.

She ran back into the bedroom, slipping a bit on the wood floor, grabbed her phone and started down the stairs. Should she tell him she wasn't ready? Take some time to look a little more, well, presentable?

She could hear his gentle knock and texted.

Cat: Costume change. Be there in a moment.

Costume change? Ugh. For someone who liked to be in control of things, this did not feel like control. At all. A hair pin tinked as it fell onto the floor.

Standing in front of her door, she looked down at herself. Well, at least the hot bath was true. Putting her hand on the doorknob, she began to turn it. Then stopped.

Magic.

Laughing, she closed her eyes, imagined what she wanted to look like and focused.

Thirty seconds later, a very calm, sexy Cat answered the door. Encased in a black satin tank top that just grazed the top of her panty line, she struck what she hoped was a sexy pose. Her red curls were artfully arranged, no signs of bath time frizz to be seen, and fell beautifully below her breasts. The redness from the pore removers was gone; her color was naturally high given the hot bath…not to mention the hot texts. Her mouth tasted of mint.

"Hey."

Devin's jaw dropped. "I thought you were kidding, that you'd be in sweats or something. Damn, Cat, you're hot enough to give this man a heart attack."

The cool wind from outside ruffled the hem of her top. Goose bumps broke out all over. Whether from the cold wind or his smoldering look, she couldn't be sure.

His gaze ran from her top to her feet. He whistled.

"What's with the cowboy boots?"

Cowboy boots?

Cat looked down. Yep, boots. Red ones. How would she explain a magical malfunction? She had nothing. At least they weren't snowshoes or bowling shoes.

"Ah, I get it. Costume change? Like role play costume stuff? You are ever a surprise, little Cat. Damn."

She had no explanation. No snappy come back, no sassy remark. Her wide green eyes took him in.

The mood shifted; she could see it in Devin's eyes. He looked at her, his eyes unable to focus on just one part—gazing at her lips, her eyes, her neck, her legs, her breasts. The sexual tension within the doorway was palpable. She felt her breathing increase, raising her shirt above her belly button with each breath. Devin ran his hand through his hair.

"Are you going to ask me in?" he finally asked, his voice husky, his body filling the frame.

A soft, quiet sound escaped from Cat. *Yes,* she thought. *This is what I want to feel like all the time.* She knew she shouldn't. She wasn't this kind of girl. They didn't even have a relationship. *But it makes that feeling go away. Doing things with him I shouldn't makes the chaos go away.*

Cat moved a few steps closer to the door, her cowboy boots tapping quietly on the wood floor. She reached out and traced his lips with one finger. She could hear his intake of breath as she continued moving her fingernails down the side of his neck and into the thick curls behind his ear.

She leaned forward and up, glad of her magically fresh breath, and placed her lips close to his without touching.

"Ask me in." Devin pleaded his hands still at his sides.

Still so close to his mouth, she whispered to him, "I want you to come inside."

Devin swore under his breath.

"I thought you'd never ask."

ABOUT THE AUTHORS

Christine Collins Cacciatore and **Jennifer Collins Starkman** started reading anything they could get their hands on at a very early age, seeking out pigs who could talk, little people who borrow or cats in the hat. It only makes sense, then, that their love of reading would flow into a love of writing.

Chris and Jenny are both married to fantastic men and have three marvelous children each, along with preposterous dogs that add to the chaos. Not to mention the most adorable grandbaby (and grandniece) who has become the Queen of the Castle.

Their lives are filled with love and laughter, and both feel blessed they are able to fulfill their dreams of writing books together.

<u>Whitfield Witch Series</u>
Book One: Baylyn, Bewitched
Book Two: Cat, Charmed
Book Three: Elise, Evermore *(coming soon)*

Made in the USA
Middletown, DE
26 February 2015